Slavery
and
Revenge

Here's what readers are saying about
"Of Chains and Slavery."

"Commander Johnson has given us an intriguing and fast-paced adventure page-turner that should be on every high schooler's required reading list; weaving together the warp of pre-revolution history with the woof of classic pirate fiction to fashion a master tapestry describing the complicated and brutal life of this new swashbuckling hero, Joshua Smoot. This novel cries out to become a major motion picture."

Doug Hawley, Owner of "Ye Landmark Collectibles" of Poulsbo, WA

"Master storyteller Roger Johnson takes us on an incredible adventure as we follow Joshua Smoot from his kidnapping from Savannah to his ultimate life as a pirate in search for the legendary Treasure of Dead Man's Chest. *"John Flint's Bastard"* has it all; high adventure, treachery, honor, gasping emotion, white-knuckled drama, all wrapped in a suspenseful story line that will not let you go. Well done, Commander Johnson!"

Robert Ceccarini, NYPD Detective Lieutenant

"An exciting adventure that transports you to another time and place. Well researched and explained. I look forward to reading more by Commander Johnson."

Joe Marek, Merrick's Privateers

"It was a genuine pleasure reading *"John Flint's Bastard."* It is an exciting blend of history and fiction during the end of the Age of Piracy and the beginning of the Age of Liberty. Make room Blackbeard, Billy the Kid, and Captain Hook, because there's a new Swashbuckler named Joshua Smoot riding the high seas."

Wade John Taylor, editor, The Pamphlet

"If you love America, you will love *"John Flint's Bastard, Slavery and Revenge,"* and the third book in this pirate adventure trilogy, *"Treasure and Redemption."* Commander Johnson spins a compelling yarn that takes place just before the American founding, and introduces us to a new swashbuckler named Joshua Smoot. A true page-turner that I could not put down. I look forward to part three."

Corey Millard, avid reader of pirate adventure

"A brilliantly painted canvas of the by-gone Golden Age of Piracy and the introduction of Joshua Smoot! Filled with intrigue, suspense, and both joyful and bitter raw emotion; Commander Johnson weaves a tale of the destiny of souls that will stir the hearts of all that read their way into this epic story! I highly recommend the trilogy!"

Penny Caldwell, author, "The God of the Mountain."

"As a child, I read and re-read Treasure Island and have hungered all these decades to learn the ultimate destination of Long John Silver and the rest of that famous treasure. That hunger has now been satisfied in Commander Johnson's trilogy, *"Of Chains and Slavery."* Written in the classic style of Robert Louis Stevenson, this fast-moving pirate novel follows the complicated life and adventures of John Flint's bastard—Joshua Smoot—from his kidnapping at Savannah, through his years as a slave, and finally to his quest for the Treasure of Dead Man's Chest. A must read for those who share my hunger."

Scott C. Kuesel, Wisconsin Maritime Historical Society

"How important is a man's identity, and what is he willing to sacrifice to keep it? These are the life-changing decisions young Joshua Smoot—the bastard son of the notorious pirate John Flint—must make. Will his odyssey break him or will he find the courage, strength, and faith to survive and conquer the life he's been forced into? The *"Of Chains and Slavery"* trilogy is a wild ride and a must read."

Michael Carver, Historical Interpreter and Reenactor

Slavery and Revenge

Of Chains and Slavery

~

A Trilogy: Part Two

Roger L. Johnson
COMMANDER, USN

SEAWORTHY PUBLICATIONS, INC. • MELBOURNE, FLORIDA

Slavery and Revenge
Of Chains and Slavery, A Trilogy: Part Two
Copyright ©2025 by Roger L. Johnson
Commander, USN
ISBN: 978-1-948494-96-0
Published in the USA by:
Seaworthy Publications, Inc.
6300 N Wickham Rd.
Unit #130-416
Melbourne, FL 32940
Phone 321-389-2506
e-mail orders@seaworthy.com
www.seaworthy.com

Library of Congress Cataloging-in-Publication Data

Names: Johnson, Roger L., Commander, author.
Title: Slavery and revenge / Roger L. Johnson, Commander, USN.
Description: Melbourne, Florida : Seaworthy Publications, Inc., 2024. |
   Series: Of chains and slavery, a trilogy ; part 2 | Summary: "Now that
   you've finished John Flint's Bastard, the first in the Of Chains and
   Slavery trilogy, it's time to reef your sails and batten down your
   hatches as you drive into this new literary storm-Slavery and
   Revenge-that will take you from the sugar plantations of Baracoa, Cuba,
   to the pirate stronghold of Tortuga, and thereafter to Charles Town,
   Savannah, and beyond where Joshua Smoot and his ragtag crew hunt down
   and exact revenge their enemies. Like John Flint's Bastard before it,
   Slavery and Revenge will drive you relentlessly onward page-by-page like
   a brigantine driven wing-and-wing before a northeaster. You'll meet
   Robert Ormerod-the man who buried The Treasure of Dead Man's Chest-and
   witness the cunning and manipulative Long John Silver as he attempts to
   acquire the L1,500,000 from that island before he dies. So, now that
   dinner is over and you have settled into your favorite chair, set sail
   for another sea adventure that is guaranteed to place Joshua Smoot as
   high in your rigging as Blackbeard, Captain Kid, Henry Every, Jack
   Rackham, and the legendary Long John Silver. And when you close the last
   page, go once again to that bookstore and buy Treasure and Redemption,
   the third in the Of Chains and Slavery trilogy"-- Provided by publisher.

Identifiers: LCCN 2024015568 (print) | LCCN 2024015569 (ebook) | ISBN
   9781948494960 (paperback) | ISBN 9781948494977 (epub)
Subjects: LCGFT: Action and adventure fiction. | Sea fiction. | Novels.
Classification: LCC PS3610.O3753 S53 2024 (print) | LCC PS3610.O3753
   (ebook) | DDC 813/.6--dc23/eng/20240404
LC record available at https://lccn.loc.gov/2024015568
LC ebook record available at https://lccn.loc.gov/2024015569

DEDICATION

I affectionately dedicate this "Of Chains and Slavery" trilogy to my wife and soul mate, Elizabeth, who has patiently endured the many months required to research and record this epic adventure of the Pirate Captain Joshua Smoot.

TABLE OF CONTENTS

FOREWORD

On November 27, 1492, the Spanish explorer Christopher Columbus landed on the island of Cuba and planted a cross on the beach and called it Cruz de la Parra in the beach. He named the place Porto Santo, and he wrote in his ships log that it was the most beautiful place he had ever seen and that his desire was to never leave the paradise. In 1511,—nineteen years later—Diego Velásquez and Hernán Cortéz sailed from Hispaniola after his attacks on the natives of the island, and landed at Cruz de la Parra where the two established a Spanish settlement that they named Baracoa. Hatuey, the Taíno tribal chief who had suffered under Velásquez and Cortéz at Hispaniola, fled in canoes with several hundred of his tribe to warn the people of Cuba what the Spaniards would do to them. According to the journal of a Catholic priest named Bartolomé, Hatuey traveled about Cuba displaying a basket of gold and jewels to the Cuban natives while telling them that this was the God that the Spaniards worshipped, and that this false God demanded that these white men from across the sea must kill and enslave his people, rob their belongings, and rape their wives and daughters. On February 2, 1512, Hatuey was captured, tied to a stake, and condemned to death by burning. When shown a crucifix and offered salvation by a Catholic priest, Hatuey asked, "Are there people like you in this heaven you describe?" When the priest assured him that there would be many like him, Hatuey answered that he would never believe in a God that would allow such cruelty to be unleashed in his name. "I would rather go to hell!"

Thus, slavery came to the islands of the Caribbean. At first, the money crops were fruits and vegetables, but within a century, tobacco and sugar plantations spread quickly across Cuba, and with them, a new level of human cruelty. During the months of harvesting and processing of the cane, men, women, and their children were forced to work twenty hours a day. To achieve control over these workers, families were separated, and these helpless and hopeless natives were forced to live in small huts called barracoons with padlocked doors and virtually no ventilation. When these people complained, they were punished by being made to stand in wooden stocks in the excruciating heat of the boiler rooms and abandoned for days without the ability to lie down. Pregnant women were beaten on their swollen bellies, often causing miscarriages. This inhumane treatment created a burning desire for freedom within the hearts and souls of the slaves. Soon, open rebellion spread across Cuba.

Slavery began with the earliest of mankind and continues to this day. Every society is guilty to a greater or lesser degree, and it is not limited to holding a person against their will or forcing them to do what they do not want to do. Although slavery was not limited to the importation of Africans to work the plantations of the Caribbean islands and the southern American states, most history books hold those two geographical regions as the rawest and most notorious manifestation of this terrible industry.

Those of us with a compassionate soul ask where such cruelty of our fellow man originated. The awful truth is that mankind is basically evil, and unless we are acted upon at an early age by some outside force to eradicate that evil within us, we grow up to behave like animals. In 1926, the Governor of Minnesota, Theodore Christenson, was so concerned with the increasing crime, established the Minnesota Crime Commission to discover the root causes of this aberrant behavior. The following is an abstract of that report written by one of the commission members. It has been quoted many times in classrooms and from pulpits across the United States.

"It must be remembered that no infant is born a finished product. On the contrary, every baby begins life as a little savage. He is equipped, among other things, with muscles and organs over which he has no control. He has an urge for self-preservation—with aggressive drives and emotions such as anger, fear, and love, over which, likewise he has practically no control. He is completely selfish and self-centered. He wants what he wants, when he wants it. His uncle's watch, his bottle, his mother's attention, or his playmate's toy. Deny him those 'wants' and he seethes with rage and aggression which would be murderous were he not so helpless. He is dirty. He has no morals, knowledge, or skills. He has no sympathy or empathy for the pain he causes others in the pursuit to satisfy his raw desires. What this means, of course, is that all children are born delinquent and if permitted to continue in the self-centered world of their infancy—and given free rein to exercise their impulsive actions to satisfy their 'wants' without the shaping of positive and negative discipline—every child would grow up a criminal, a thief, a killer, and a rapist. In the process of growing up, it is completely normal for every child to be dirty, to fight, to grab, to steal, to tear things apart, to talk back to parents, and to evade. Every child must—through the parent's use of a loving system of rewards and punishment—be forced to grow out of his delinquent behavior. This is the parent's God-ordained responsibility."

There is nothing that incompetence hates more than virtue, and there exists an enormous social industry that supports maturity retardation. The psychologists and lawyers have perfected the fine art of rationalization, explanations, and excuses for those who never matured beyond that adolescent state. Through several means—with political correctness at the top of the list—these so-called *'learned men and women of psychology'* have convinced society that people who have done wrong should not be held to account for their bad behavior—that they are not culpable or guilty. Rather—theirs was a mistake, a sickness, or a syndrome, a habit, an addiction, and not a moral fault or transgression. In a myriad of ways, we train ourselves to avoid, evade, or explain why we do not bear responsibility for our bad behavior.

It is from this irresponsible and aberrant leadership, the love of money, and the resulting behavior that we get the cruelty of slavery and the destructive acts of revenge when those who are victimized eventually strike back. Regardless of what it is called, at its core, it is revenge.

In the year 1846, French author Eugene Sue published a book titled Memoirs of Matilda in which he wrote the phrase, *"And then revenge is very good eaten cold, as the vulgar say."* The phrase has been shortened to *"Revenge is a dish best served cold,"* and appears often in various novels, stage plays, and motion pictures.

Our criminal law system tells us that there are three primary motives for murder—money, love, and revenge. But, if you think about those three, something becomes vividly apparent. When somebody cheats us out of our money, we contemplate revenge. When the person we love is harmed or killed, we contemplate revenge. Love and money are the crimes, while revenge is the compensation we desire for that crime. This overpowering urge for revenge is the natural reaction to an unjust injury, especially for the murder of a loved one.

Envy and revenge was the reason for the very first instance of murder in the Bible. In Genesis chapter four we read how Cain took revenge and killed his brother Able over jealousy for their parent's approval. And in Exodus, revenge lifts its ugly head over and over, and is even spelled out in detail in Exodus 21: 23-25. "And if any mischief follows, then thou shalt give life for life, eye for eye, tooth for tooth, hand for hand, foot for foot, burning for burning, wound for wound, and stripe for stripe."

Joshua Smoot had suffered repeated attacks and cruelty by nearly every person he had met, beginning with his kidnapping from Savannah by John Flint, his slave-like treatment by Lord Lyddell at Wakehurst Place in England, and culminating with Edwin Drake forcing Rebecca Keyes to either watch Joshua be hung from a yardarm or sent away as a slave.

Now, with their ankles tied to the anchor of the slave ship *Crow*, the two slaves—Joshua and the Ethiopian Jew Simbatu—stand balanced on the gunwale waiting to be dragged to the bottom of Baracoa Harbor.

CHAPTER ONE:
Anchored to Slavery

When Joshua Smoot woke up from being knocked unconscious, he found himself naked and shackled next to the Ethiopian Jew, Simbatu. Now, instead of scraping and swabbing the human waste from the slave platforms, Joshua was a part of that disgusting display of man's inhumanity to his fellow man.

Seaman Parker stepped down the ladder, walked to Joshua, and stood at his feet. "Good! I see that they didn't hit you hard enough to kill you."

"Parker!" Joshua struggled up onto an elbow and looked at his friend. "What does Captain Sperry intend for me?"

"His intention was to simply kill you, but I convinced him that he should fulfill Captain Drake's wish that you be sold at Baracoa."

"I could hear the crew preparing for something. Is that what is happening? Are we nearing Baracoa?"

"Yes—just entering the bay now." He held up his key. "I've been sent to take you and your African friend topside."

"Just the two of us?" He looked across the platform at the other slaves. "None of these others are being sold here?"

"Just you two." While he unlocked the shackles, Parker looked around to make certain they were alone. "Once we get on deck, it is important that you pay attention to everything I do and say."

"What are you going to do and say?"

"You two are being tied to the anchor and dragged to the bottom of the bay." Joshua's shackle opened. "Your lives—yours and this Africans life—depend on what you see and hear."

☠ ☠ ☠

1

Joshua and Simbatu were led up the ladder and into the morning sunlight. Parker pointed at two shirts and two pairs of trousers thrown on the deck. "Get dressed."

Joshua turned to the African. "I don't know if this is to be a good thing or a bad thing, but either way, you are right. I did this to us."

"It is God's will, my friend, so there is no blame."

With the luffing of her sails, the *Crow* came to a stop in the harbor a hundred yards from the waterfront. Captain Sperry walked forward to the three men. "Parker! Are they ready?"

"Aye, Captain!"

"I see you have your rope, so get to it."

Parker picked up the first of two hemp ropes. While he made the familiar loop and folded the two halves onto themselves to form the transom knot, he stepped to Joshua. "Raise your foot, Manley."

"What are you doing?"

"I'm tying a transom knot around your foot, and I am going to tie the other end to the anchor with a bowline." He snugged the knot and repeated the process with Simbatu. While the two watched, Parker passed the two ropes out over the rail and back to the anchor. "There—just like the day I pulled you from the chain locker and gave you that seawater bath."

Joshua turned to Captain Sperry. "You're going to drown us?"

"I'm going to send you to the bottom of this bay. Whether you drown or not will depend on you."

"Are we worth so little to you?"

"Are you begging me for mercy, John Manley?"

"Yes—if that will save our lives."

"But what sort of a message would that give to the rest of my crew?" He looked about at the men who had gathered to watch the spectacle. "All ships captains depend on loyalty from their men, and the way they foster that loyalty varies from one ship to the next. I read a book once that told me that it is better for a leader to be feared than to be loved." He took the time to look from one man to the next. "You men are watching me, as you should be." He pointed behind him to Joshua and Simbatu. "If I let John Manley go without the punishment that I warned him he would receive, every one of you would remember my leniency, and you would then question every order I give from this day forward. Such questioning of my authority always leads to mutiny."

"Isn't selling us here—at Baracoa—punishment enough?"

"No!" He turned back to Joshua. "You understood and agreed to my order to never befriend any of these slaves, and that it would bring harm upon you. For disobeying that order, you and your African will suffer the harm you brought upon yourself."

"I'll take the cat—the stripes both Simbatu and I deserve—if it will change your mind."

"You'd do that for an African slave?"

"I did this. I disobeyed your order. Not him."

"But you are ignoring the way it works between a pet and his master."

"What?" He looked at Simbatu and back to the captain. "I don't understand."

"A pet always follows his master, and you were warned to never make one of these Africans your pet." He stepped close. "If your African drowns, it is because he followed you to the bottom of the bay."

"All he did was say my name."

"Your hands are free, John Manley. If you can hold your breath long enough to untie those knots before your lungs suck themselves full of sea water, then you will live. If not, then you will die."

One of the sailors called. "Your boat is ready, Captain!"

"Then it's time that we drop anchor." He turned back to Joshua and Simbatu. "I will be waiting at the beach to see whether you and your pet African survive."

While the captain walked aft, Parker gave Joshua a nudge. "The anchor will pull you up and over the rail with enough force to break your leg. You best climb up onto the rail and jump as it falls into the water."

"Yes—you're right." Joshua and Simbatu climbed up onto the gunwale and used each other for balance as two of the crew readied to release the anchor.

"I can't swim, Joshua."

"Then your only hope is to take the largest breath you have ever taken and pray for help from your God." As he said the last word, the mallet struck the keeper and the anchor dropped into the water, dragging the two slaves from the rail.

The anchor pulled Joshua and Simbatu downward through the crystal-clear water of Baracoa Bay with the force of a demon taking two lost souls to hell—dragging the helpless young men so fast that even though they tried with all their might, neither could reach down to their ankle and the vicious constrictor knot that held them. While his ear drums were compressed by the building pressure, Joshua could only watch and wait for the anchor to finally reach the bottom six fathoms below. Once on the bottom, the anchor turned on its side allowing one of the great flukes to dig deeply into the rocks and coral. A moment later, the chain pulled taut against the drifting ship.

Joshua's fingers hurt, as did the rest of his body. As Parker had warned, the transom knot about his ankle would not give. *The bowline!* With his lungs burning from the build-up of carbon dioxide, and his ear drums ready to burst inward from the tremendous pressure at over thirty feet, he pulled himself down to the anchor and began working at the bowline. *Oh, God—if you are there—please help us out of this hell that my disobedience has put us in!*

While he turned the knot around, Simbatu pulled down next to him and began beating at his ankle as if that would cause the knot to loosen. Joshua turned from his own bowline and released Simbatu to the surface.

With his lungs screaming for oxygen, Joshua turned back to his knot. With a quick push, the top broke loose and the knot untied. Joshua set his feet against the coral head and gave a tremendous push, driving him upward. Thirty feet... twenty feet...ten feet. For a moment, the sea turned dark, as if a candle had been snuffed in a dark room. He did not remember taking the breaths, but a moment later, as his senses returned, the sound of gasping and splashing came to his ears. It was Simbatu struggling to stay afloat.

"Take and hold the biggest breath you can!" Joshua grabbed the African's hair and tried to turn him away. "It will make you float while I pull you to shore!"

The African thrashed about in the water oblivious of what Joshua had told him.

"Do what I told you or—"

The African spun around and grabbed Joshua by the face while trying to climb atop him, driving both under the surface. As they emerged, Joshua balled up his fist and drove it at Simbatu's chin with all the strength he could muster. Now, with the African unconscious, Joshua rolled him onto his back, grabbed his hair, and dragged him through the water toward the beach. When they reached the shallows, Simbatu regained his senses.

"Why did you hit me?"

"Because you would have drowned both of us." Joshua turned and crawled to the rocky beach where he collapsed face down.

"Well, well!" Captain Sperry stepped to Joshua and gave him a kick to the shoulder. "You just made me lose a sovereign to each of my men, John Manley."

Joshua turned onto his back and looked up. "If I was a free man and I had a weapon, it would cost you more than two sovereigns."

Sperry put a hand on his pistol. "Ah, you tempt me." He turned to his two men. "Bring them."

One of the seamen grabbed the two slaves by the hair and pulled them to their feet. "Your choice" He pointed. "Walk, or we'll drag you up to the town by your ropes."

Once on his feet, Joshua stumbled about for a moment. "Where are you taking us?"

Captain Sperry called back. "Take them to the slave cage while I bargain with Gordo!"

While the two were shoved into the cage, Captain Sperry walked to a two-story abode building. He stopped under the portico and looked back to make sure his two seamen had obeyed his order. Satisfied, he disappeared into the building.

"Here!" The seamen held the end of the rope. "You two can keep your ropes. Maybe you can find a place to tie it so you can finish the job the anchor didn't."

The captain returned with a fat man dressed in party clothes. The man stepped to the cage and poked at Joshua with a sharp stick. "Stretch out so I can see your arms and legs!"

"No!"

"I am Ricardo El Arriaga!" He put his hands on his fat belly. "Some call me Gordo." He looked at the note Captain Sperry gave him and at Joshua. "I own you now, John Manley—body, soul, and spirit—along with this African. This is Baracoa, so I can sell you two on the auction block or I can kill you! Nobody will care either way."

Joshua straightened his legs and turned his arms so his palms showed.

"Hmm Not so good." Gordo turned to Captain Sperry. "The white one seems sound enough, except for that scar on his hand and the one across his face."

"The scars gives him character, and since you're such a good liar, you could make up a fantastic story about how he got them." The captain could see that his property was losing its value by the moment. "It proves he's a fighter."

"It looks like he fought and lost." The fat man shook his head. "The ladies prefer that their slaves have pretty faces." He pulled a handful of coins from his coat pocket and fingered through them. "Forty sovereigns for the white one and thirty for the black one."

It took the captain a moment. "Well, since I paid nothing for the white one, I'll take the seventy for the two of them."

Gordo looked to the *Crow*. "I could use a few breeders—young and strong girls—if you have any extra."

"What would you pay for them?"

"Twenty each."

"No. They pay me double that at the other ports."

"A man has to try, doesn't he?"

☠ ☠ ☠

The slave cage measured four spans wide and long and was built from giant bamboo tied together with rawhide strips. Because of the stench of the ground that was more dung than dirt, it sat near a cliff at the lee edge of town so that the stench blew out to sea.

After several minutes alone, Simbatu reached down and touched the transom knot at his ankle. "Why did you do that?"

"What?"

"You started to untie yourself from the anchor, but you stopped and untied me first. Why did you do that?"

"I…" It took Joshua a moment to answer. "If you had drowned, your death would be on me." He paused. "I am alone and I have nobody but you."

"Then you are not holding this against me—that I said your name and caused this?"

"I already told you that this was my fault. I was the one who disobeyed the captain's order, not you."

"Those things the captain said when he caught us talking, and the things he said to his crewmen just before we were pulled into the water. Do you agree with those things?"

"What things?"

"That I am an animal—just livestock like cattle or sheep—and that I don't have a soul." He waited. "He said that I am not a person. Do you agree with what he said?"

"I don't know."

"But you untied me before you untied yourself. And now you claim me as the only person you have."

"I didn't call you a person."

"You told me that you have nobody but me. That makes me somebody, and I have never heard anybody call his livestock somebody."

"Well, since you can speak English, and since you can think like me, then I suppose you might be a man."

"Just before Captain Sperry caught us talking, you were going to tell me what brought you to the *Crow* as a slave."

"It started in Savannah where I was born."

"So, you had a family like me."

"My name is Joshua Smoot. I have an older sister, and my mother was one of several midwives. Her name was Emily Smoot."

"Why do you say was when you named your mother?"

"She was killed when I was eight by a pirate named John Flint. He forced my sister and me to watch."

"Go on."

"Before she was killed, my mother told me that she was not my real mother—the woman who birthed me—that my real mother was a woman named Elaine MacBride. She told me that John Flint took her from my real father during a raid on their ship and brought her to Savannah to be his…"

"Yes—I know what pirates do with women they capture."

"Emily told me that I was the son of David and Elaine MacBride of Scotland, but when I was eight, John Flint told me that was a lie—that he was my father."

"On the *Crow*, they called you John Manley. What did John Flint name you?"

"Thomas Flint, but I never agreed to the name, and that caused everybody to treat me like a slave."

"Everybody?"

"Flint took me to a man in England who was supposed to raise me as a gentleman. He told the man that he could punish me any way he wanted if I refused my new name."

"Yes?"

"I refused, and I was sent to the stables as punishment, but I liked the work. For over ten years I never changed my name."

"Then why aren't you still in England?"

"I did what Captain Sperry said a man should never do. I made one of the horses my pet. Her name was Emily—the same as the woman who raised me."

"Hmm."

"My horse got sick, and Lord Lyddell said that he would let her die if I didn't change my name." He raised his hands. "I tried to kill him, and then I was told that Emily was to be slaughtered and eaten if I did not become Thomas Flint. The stable master broke me out and I fled the place with Emily."

Simbatu gave a laugh.

"What?"

"John, Manley, Joshua, Smoot, Thomas, and Flint—a man with six different names."

"I have only one name, and it is Joshua Smoot."

"Then Joshua Smoot is a fool."

"John Flint killed my mother in front of me. I made up my mind that I would never take his name."

"But it was only a name. A man is more than what he is called."

"But *your* name meant so much to you, and you changed it from Batu to Simbatu."

"Yes." Simbatu nodded. "I changed my name as punishment for the shame that haunts me." He reached out and touched Joshua's face. "That scar on your face is fresh. Was it the Englishman who did that to you?"

"Yes." Joshua nodded and rubbed the scar. "I foolishly returned to visit my friends, and Lord Lyddell shot me. After a nice lady sewed my face back together, I followed Becky—the girl I loved and wanted to marry—north to a town called Lambeth where we indentured ourselves for passage to Charles Town."

"So, it wasn't Lord Lyddell who sold you into slavery?"

"No, that happened after we were at sea." Joshua gave a frustrated huff. "The solicitor had a list of those with the King's warrants on them. The only way I could go with Becky was to choose another name."

"John Manley?"

"He was the stable master where I was kept all those years."

"So, you and Becky boarded a ship as free people bound for America."

"The ship was the *Maiden*, and the captain told us that once at sea, he would marry us."

"Let me guess." Simbatu leaned forward slightly. "Somebody else on the *Maiden* had eyes for Becky."

"It was the captain's son, and he provoked me to fight him for Becky's honor. When I had my knife at his throat, I was knocked senseless, and when I woke up, I had a noose around my throat."

"Oh, Lord."

"I was to be hanged immediately, but Becky pleaded for my life." Joshua touched his throat. "Captain Drake gave her the choice—that I be sent here as a slave or be hanged while she was forced to watch."

"A terrible choice."

"If I am ever free, I will hunt for Captain Drake and his son. When I find them, I will kill them."

"I am a slave because I was a coward. You are a slave because you were fighting for the woman you loved."

"That scar on your hand. Did somebody nail you to a board?"

"This happened when I was being taken to England. John Flint held me out over the passing sea while he threatened to feed me to the sharks. But rather than drop me into the sea, he threw me to the man who had cared for me. I fell to the deck and my chain began dragging me back to the sea just like that anchor today. Just before I went over the side, he threw a pike and pinioned my hand to the deck."

"Then he must not have hated you as much as you believed."

"I was told that same day that John Flint was aiming for my heart."

"It is still God's will that you lived and that we are now here at Baracoa together."

"If there is a God, he didn't send us here because he loves us." Joshua spread his arms. "This is hatred—pure hatred."

"No, my friend." Simbatu shook his head. "Sometimes love seems like hatred, but later when we look back on it, we see the good that God intended."

"By making us slaves?"

"It is a blessing that he has done so."

"How can this be a blessing?"

"I have been told slaves do better here than bondsmen."

"Why?"

"Slaves are a life-long investment, while the bondsmen are here for only a few years. If a bondsman gets sick or injured, the overseer will allow him to die, but since we will be their personal property, they won't kill us unless we force them to."

CHAPTER TWO:
The Sugar Plantation

Sunday morning looked like any other day at Baracoa, Cuba, except for those who passed the slave cage on foot or in their polished enameled carriages. The children amused themselves by mocking and poking sticks at the two new slaves, while their parents pretended indifference on this day set aside for religion.

Joshua and Simbatu watched the couples enter the Catholic Church and then emerge two hours later. Now that they had paid homage to their God, they all made certain to walk past the cage for a look at the two new slaves. While the men muttered and nodded, the women covered their mouths and noses with their kerchiefs and looked at the two with feigned disgust. One of the women nodded at Joshua and whispered something to her husband. He touched his left cheek and shook his head. When the wife objected, the man nodded back and stepped to Ricardo El Arriaga while his wife studied the young white slave. "Good morning, Gordo."

The fat man gave a curt bow. "Good morning, Don Santana." He looked to his two prisoners. "It is cultivation time, is it not?"

The man nodded. "When will these two be put on the block?"

The fat man gave a polite laugh. "Not until I get at least ten more, but as you know, I am always willing to rent out my slaves until that day." He nodded at the man's wife. "Your beautiful wife seems interested in these two. Why not test them now to see if they are worth bidding on."

"At the usual price?" The Don gave Gordo a suspicious look. "A dollar a week?"

The fat man licked his lips. "If it were any other time besides the harvest, I would agree to that amount, but slaves are worth more at this time of year."

"Don't play with me, Gordo. Name your price."

"Two dollars a week."

"No." The Don took his wife's hand and pulled her away from the cage. "We're going home."

"Wait!" The fat man gave the planter a flat look. "I will agree to three dollars for two weeks, and you can have both of them." He held up a hand. "But you must return them with no sign of punishment on their bodies."

"What if they refuse my factor's orders? Are you saying he is not allowed to punish them?"

"If they are trouble, bring them back and I will return your money."

The man looked back at his wife. The stench of the slaves repulsed her, but she uncovered her mouth just enough to mouth her silent approval.

Don Santana turned back to the slaver. "Have them cleaned up. I will send Alazar to collect them in the morning."

☠ ☠ ☠

Early Monday morning at sunrise, the two slaves were marched down to the bay. While Don Santana's factor watched, Gordo marched Joshua and Simbatu down to the bay. "You both stink of the dung-filled dirt." He pointed." Go out into the water, strip naked, and wash your bodies and your clothes." It took only minutes, and then the two were led up the beach to the factor's horse cart.

"My name is Alazar. I am Don Santana's factor. That is how you will address me—Factor." The man was a Muslim Arab who was darkly tanned from his life outdoors and stood over six feet tall. He wore a loose-fitting shirt and a wide-brimmed hat that was woven from grass.

"While you are working for me, I will be your mother, I will be your father, and I will be your God. You will stand when I tell you to stand. You will sit when I tell you to sit. Likewise, you will eat and drink when I say to do so. If you do not obey me, you will be punished."

Joshua pointed at the fat slave trader. "Gordo said you can't beat us—that the marks on our body will make us worth less on the slave block."

Simbatu cringed.

Alazar stepped toward Joshua. "Oh, he did, did he?"

"Please!" Simbatu stepped in front of Joshua. "My young friend is a half-wit. He is new to this life and does not understand yet what it means to be a slave." He gave Joshua a sharp punch to the gut that sent the young man to his knees. "I will teach him."

"Joshua?" Alazar stepped to the young white man. "I thought your name was John Manley."

"My real name is Joshua Smoot. I had to change it to leave England."

"Very well, Joshua Smoot." He looked to Simbatu and back to Joshua. "Don Santana will always know you as John Manley."

The Muslim stepped to Simbatu and stood nose to nose. "My employer told me that you are an Ethiopian Jew who claims to be a Christian." The factor gave a laugh. "Maybe I will punish you in this white man's place if he disobeys me, like you believe Jesus did for you on that Roman cross." Alazar turned to his cart, picked the leather manacles, and applied them to the men's wrists. He climbed into the cart, gave the horse a twitch with the whip, and called out. "Walk on!"

At first the cart traveled at a walking speed, but once the horse left the soft sand and gained the solid ground of the town street, it increased to a trot, forcing the two men to run for several miles. After what seemed like ten miles, the factor stopped the cart at a watering trough. The horse drank its fill and then Alazar pulled the cart forward so the two slaves could reach the trough.

Simbatu filled his hands with the filthy water and closed his eyes. "Thank you, Lord."

Joshua stopped drinking and turned to the African. "How can you thank God for this filth?"

"It is because Jesus told us that every time we eat or drink, the food and the water are daily reminders of what He did for us on the cross."

"I can't do that."

"I will pray that someday you will believe in my God—the God Abraham, Isaac, and Jacob. The God who created heaven and earth. The same God who parted the Red Sea so His people could go to His mountain in Midian."

"But, you're black. Isn't the God you are describing the white man's God?"

"He's the God of all men and all tribes. He is the only God and Creator."

"But you heard what Captain Sperry told me about your kind."

The black man laughed. "Do you believe Captain Sperry's lie that I am nothing but an animal—your pet—that I must be broke of both my freedom and its memory, just like a beast of burden?"

"From what has happened to me since I left England, I'm not sure what to believe anymore."

"Know this, Joshua." He looked to Alazar and lowered his voice. "You and I are alike in that we both came to this place as free men."

"And?"

"It means that whoever buys us knows that we are trouble because we are not like the second and third generation slaves who never knew such freedom. They will have their factors watch us for any sign of sedition."

"If we are so dangerous, why don't they just kill us?"

"If we were indentured servants, they would. But since they will own us, they will take other means to control us."

"How so?"

"They will breed us and then they will separate us from our women and our children so that we cannot teach the little ones about freedom."

"But the mothers will remember and teach the children."

"No! After our kind are separated from them, the women will have no support and will raise the children to be good little slaves."

"I don't know whether either of us has a soul, but neither of us is an animal to be broken and turned into a beast of burden." Joshua raised his hands from the water. "These restraints—"

Before Joshua could finish, Alazar laid the whip to the gelding and the two were jerked violently sideways from the water trough and back to a run. Alazar called back at the two. "If you want to talk, do it while you are running."

The plantation started at the watering trough. After several more miles, the factor reined the horse to a stop in a large clearing where two dozen men were cutting cane while others delivered and unloading the stalks near a large fire. Others—mostly women—were stripping the leaves from the cane and throwing them onto the fire.

The factor removed Simbatu's and Joshua's restraints and pointed at the fire. "You will begin by stripping off the leaves and throwing them onto the fire. This will be your job until I can trust you to not run away."

Joshua rubbed his wrists. "What will we do after that?"

"You will be allowed to cut cane with the other slaves."

The two worked for only an hour at the fires when Joshua held his hands out to the African. His blood dripped from his fingertips, mingled with his sweat. "This is terrible! Look at my hands!"

"I am bleeding too, Joshua." He looked to the women. "They are doing it without getting cut. We will learn."

Out of necessity and the need for survival, Joshua quickly learned how to pull the long leaves loose from the cane stalks without being cut. When the first day finally came to a merciful end, the two dozen male slaves and bondsmen were gathered for the walk to the sleeping area where a group of women were preparing food. There were ten circular huts, each measuring two spans wide. The roofs were of woven grass with walls of mud spread over and through the thumb-size sticks that were woven together basket-fashion. The women had already eaten their portion and left the pot and bowls on crude tables for the arriving men.

Alazar drove his cart to the center of the men's stockade and turned it about next to the table. While the slaves and bondsmen trotted to a stop some distance from the tables, Alazar's horse began to munch from one of the platters of cooked greens.

"After you eat, I would advise you to find an empty cot in one of those huts and sleep as much as you are able. If you are lucky enough to dream, know that those places of goodness and freedom that your dreams offer only exist in your imaginations and memories. You will never see freedom again." With that, Alazar reigned the horse away from the table, and with a twitch of his whip, drove out of the compound, and was gone.

After three days at the fires, Alazar handed Joshua and Simbatu their knives and pointed at the wall of sugar cane a hundred yards away. "Cut the cane low to the ground and load it onto the hand carts as the others are doing." He gave the two a slight smile. "You may think cutting is a better job, but the cane snakes will make you wish you were back at the fires doing the women's work."

CHAPTER THREE:
Of Cholera and Fire

The days were long, the temperature was high, and the humidity was relentless. The slaves were brought water once each hour but were offered nothing for the small cuts that covered their hands and forearms.

On the second day of cutting, Joshua heard a man cry out in pain. He stopped cutting and ran to see what had happened—fearing that the man had cut himself. What he found turned his blood to fire. Alazar had the man on the ground and was whipping him unmercifully with his cat. The man was begging for forgiveness as he squirmed about trying to protect himself, but Alazar would not stop. Joshua ran up behind the factor and grabbed several of the strands of the cat on the backswing. Alazar spun on Joshua, just as Simbatu rounded a stand of cane from the other side.

"How dare you?" Alazar jerked at the cat, but Joshua held firm.

"He's already learned his lesson! There's no need to continue beating him except for meanness!"

"You're right, Joshua Smoot! He has learned his lesson!" Alazar gave the cat another firm jerk and Joshua let go. "But you haven't learned your lesson yet!" Alazar raised the whip to strike Joshua, but then he spotted Simbatu. "Well, well, what have we here?"

"Simbatu is no part of this. Leave him alone."

"But he's a Christian and I've heard him bragging about how his Jesus sacrificed himself for everybody in the world, and how that was such a good thing." He looked at Simbatu and pointed at Joshua. "John Manley deserves a punishment for interfering with that man's whipping, so I am going to let you play Jesus by suffering in his place." Alazar walked to the large Black man and circled him. "Not a single stripe on either of you yet, and I've been ordered to keep it that way." The factor pointed to several pieces of cane lying nearby. "Line those up next to each other and three inches apart."

"Why? What are going to do to him?"

The factor pointed down at the cane. "On your knees, Simbatu, on top of the cane."

Simbatu looked at Joshua and back to Alazar.

Alazar pointed the pistol from his sash and pointed it at Simbatu. "Down, or I will shoot you and tell Don Santana that you attacked me."

Two hours later, Alazar summoned Joshua to the place of torture. Simbatu knelt silent and hunched forward as if in prayer. Spit, mucus, and tears streamed from his face onto his legs and the ground in front of him. While Joshua watched, Alazar gave the near unconscious Negro a vicious kick to the shoulder that sent him sprawling to the ground next to the cane.

The Muslim bent down over the gasping man. "Tell me, *Christian*. Do you *still* believe in your God—that he sacrifices himself for you?"

Simbatu turned his head and looked up at the silhouetted factor. "Would a man stop believing in water if it drowned him? Would a man stop believing in the sun if it burned his skin?" He nodded. "My God does not need my belief to be there."

"This was good." Alazar turned and looked at Joshua. "Next time, John Manley will suffer in your place."

☠ ☠ ☠

"Alazar!" It was the fourth day of cutting. Joshua called again. "Alazar! I need to talk to you!"

"What?" The factor walked to Joshua and looked at his bleeding hands. "I knew it. You cut yourself and now you want to go back to the women's work at the fires."

Joshua spread his arms. "Why don't you set fire to the field and burn away the leaves before it is cut? It would make the harvest go much quicker."

"Set fire to the standing cane?" He looked around. "It would destroy the crop."

Joshua shook his head. "I tried it when I was stripping leaves. I thrust a stalk of cane into the fire. The leaves burned away, but the stalk was only blackened. When I cut the cane open, the inside was untouched."

Alazar looked at the standing stalks. "Come." Joshua followed Alazar to the fires and stopped next to one of the carts. "Do it. Show me how it works."

Joshua pulled several stalks from the cart and threw them onto the fire. The leaves burst into flame and were consumed within seconds. Alazar started to pull the stalks from the flames, but Joshua stopped him.

"Let them burn a little longer, just like they would if the whole field was burning. That's the only way to know for sure it will work." After another minute, Joshua pulled the stalks out, let them cool for a moment, and then selected one. "Look." He cut the cane open with his knife and stripped off the blackened outside. He took another piece that had not been burned and cut it the same way. He held the two out to the factor. "See? You can't tell which one was burned."

"The only way to know whether this will truly work is by burning a small portion of the field." Alazar looked around and spotted a stand of cane approximately three spans on a side. He pointed. "There! We'll burn that one."

With several workers standing near with buckets of water to make sure that the fire would not spread to the main field, Alazar turned to Joshua. "Go ahead—set the fire."

It took a moment to get the first leaves started, but in a matter of minutes, the fire had raced upward to the tops of the stalks and across the small stand, consuming all the leaves in its path. As predicted, the fire extinguished itself when the leaves were gone. Joshua cut down a stalk and brought it over to the cart.

"There!" Joshua repeated the cuts the same as before and handed it to Alazar. "It's just like the one I burned on this fire."

Alazar bit into the sweet pulp and then looked around at Joshua. He gave a smile. "It worked. You were right."

"Will you tell your master that it was my idea?"

"Of course, I will."

Three days later, Alazar drove his horse cart into the slave's compound and shouted for everybody to get up. One by one, the men emerged from the huts. It was the day Joshua and Simbatu had been waiting for.

"Word has come from town that a ship arrived last night with a dozen more slaves." He looked at Simbatu and Joshua. "My master—Don Santana—has directed me to take you two back to Gordo's cage at Baracoa to be sold with the new arrivals."

Auction day brought all the plantation owners to the town—some to buy slaves and others to watch the spectacle. Alazar had already convinced Don Santana to buy Joshua and Simbatu. The bidding had reached two-hundred pounds when Don Santana held up a leather bag of gold coins and made his single bid. "Five hundred for the two!"

Knowing that nobody in the crowd would bid against Don Santana, Gordo called out. "Sold for five-hundred pounds!"

☠ ☠ ☠

Life changed for Joshua and Simbatu after the auction. They were taken back to the same plantation and put under the same cruel factor. The work was the same, but now that they were the property of Don Santana, Alazar was free to increase both the frequency and severity of the punishment he meted out for the smallest infraction.

During the third week of their life at the Santana plantation, there was a commotion in the huts of the indentured men. One of the men was at the gate calling for help.

Joshua sat up and gave Simbatu a shake. "Something's wrong. Someone is calling Alazar for help."

"It must be that man who was bitten by the snake."

"Stay here. I'm going to see what is going on." A moment later, Joshua reached the compound gate where one of the slaves was standing naked with dung streaming down his legs. "What's wrong?"

"I'm sick, and there are men in two of the other huts just as bad as me." The man pointed at his hut. "It's cholera. We're going to die."

Joshua knew about the disease and backed away. "Not everybody dies when they catch this disease. There are medicines that help."

"Then help me get Alazar to give us those medicines."

Joshua turned to call with the sick man as Alazar approached the gate with his short whip. "What is going on? Why aren't you two sleeping?"

"There's cholera." Joshua pointed to the man. "This man and several others in those far huts are infected. They need medicine."

"It's quinine they need and we don't have any." Alazar pointed to Joshua's hut with his whip. "What about your hut? Is anybody sick?"

"No."

"Then go back and sleep. You have a full day tomorrow."

"They'll die if they don't get help."

"So?"

"You don't care?"

"Care?" Alazar covered his nose and mouth with his sleeve. "Of course, I care, but my concern and being able to do something about it are two different things."

"Cholera spreads quickly, and it will serve you right if we all die, Alazar. Don Santana will have your head if you allow that."

"Very well. I will do something." He pointed at the huts. Wake the uninfected slaves and bring them to the gate." Alazar gave Joshua a poke with his whip handle. "Now!"

Five minutes later, Alazar loaded the eight unaffected men onto his cart and drove them across the plantation, over an area of open land, and down a narrow gulley to a cove at the ocean's edge. The sandy beach was two-hundred feet wide at the water line, and bound in by a steep cliff to the east and the west.

Alazar gave Joshua a rough push to make him catch up with the others. "There is no way of escape from this cove except past this guard or to the sharks that feed at the reef." He pointed to the sea. "Of course, you can try to swim to Hispaniola or to Jamaica." Alazar pulled the guard forward and pointed at Joshua. "Watch this man, Pedro. His name is John Manley, and he is their ringleader. If there is trouble, shoot him first."

"You want me to shoot John?"

"Yes." He pointed. "Then shoot the big African they call Simbatu. He is also a leader."

"Wait!" Joshua stepped back a pace. "We have no food or water."

"I will send what you need in the morning. In the meantime, find yourselves a place to lie down, and thank your God that you are not sick."

"What about those men you left at the compound?"

"They are not your concern. If I choose to lock them inside their huts and burn them down, what is that to you?"

"You're serious—that you would do that to those men?"

"Yes. Those men are already dead. They just don't know it."

CHAPTER FOUR:
The Long Boat

O nce Alazar left, Simbatu stepped to Joshua. "What was that? What did Alazar tell you?"

"He told me that he will send food and water to us tomorrow morning."

"What about those others—the infected ones that were left at the compound?"

"He said that he might burn their huts down with them trapped inside."

"On, no!" Simbatu looked toward he sea and back to Joshua. "How long will we be kept on this beach?"

"I don't know." Joshua shook his head. "Cholera is spread by bad food and water. It will take some time to purge the kitchen and find a cleaner water supply."

"Then we could be here for several days."

"I don't know what tomorrow holds, Simbatu, any more than you." He looked north to the sea. "The ocean represents freedom. Maybe your God will open the sea like he did for Moses so we can walk to America."

"The only way to freedom is if we swim, but I don't know how to swim. Even if we could get to another beach to the east or west of here, Alazar and his men would search until they find us."

"Then there is no hope for us, my friend." He turned and looked at the six others. "We might as well get some rest and hope none of us come down with the disease."

Within an hour of sunset, Pedro was fast asleep with his rifle across his chest. Joshua spent a fitful night and was up and exploring the perimeter of their prison as the sun was beginning to pink the eastern sky. To the north was the surf line that lapped at the crabs that ran back and forth in the surging water. To the west was a sheer cliff with only small bushes cluttered at its base. To the east was another cliff where three palms stretched out over the water.

"Coconuts!" Joshua stood at the waterline and counted six of the green fruit. "Food and water!" He looked around at the rocks, trying to find one sharp enough to tear through the hard husks. He studied the rocks beyond the edge of the cliff and spotted several broken shards that had fallen onto an outcropping twenty yards past the end of the beach. With a look to seaward to make sure there were no sharks, he waded into the water to his armpits and made his way around the point. As he approached the flat rock, he heard hollow wood bumping against the rocks.

"A boat!" Partially wedged between several large rocks and the thick undergrowth, a ship's boat of three spans was tied to the rocks. Joshua waded to its edge and looked inside. The four oars were there, and the sail looked to be intact. "Yes!"

Joshua waded back around the cliff and ran up the beach to the others. He dropped to his knees, gave Simbatu a nudge, and whispered. "Your God has given us a means of escape!"

"What?" The African rubbed the sand from his face and blinked up at his friend. "What did you say?"

"Do you remember those two men that Alazar caught stealing from Don Santana's hacienda—the two they made us watch while they executed them?"

"Yes?"

"I think they came in a boat that is tied to the rocks just beyond that point."

"Then…?"

"Your God must have sent them here so that we could have a way of escape." Joshua looked to the guard to make sure he was still sleeping. "Wake the others." He pointed to the west end of the beach. "Take them down to the water line and wait while I brush away my tracks."

As silently as possible, Simbatu woke the others and cautioned them to be quiet. He looked around to where Joshua was nearing the water.

"What are we doing, Simbatu?" It was one of the younger men. "Why have you woken us so early?"

"Keep your voices down, get up, and walk down to the west end of the beach. I'll tell you why when you get there."

With his sweeping finished, Joshua followed the other's footprints and stepped into the ankle-deep water. "Listen up. There is a boat tied to the rocks at the other end of the beach." He pointed, and then turned around to the west. "When Alazar discovers that we are gone, he will follow the tracks you just left in the sand."

"You're taking us to sea?" It was Tyler—one of the younger men.

"It's that or we go back to the plantation and die like the others?"

"At least back there we have food and water." He pointed seaward. "Out there we have nothing."

"Simbatu and I are going." Joshua turned to Tyler. "I will not force any of you to do this but be warned. Alazar will torture you to find out where we went." He gave Tyler a poke to the chest. "If you choose to stay and face that, then do us a favor by telling Alazar that when you woke up, we were gone—that you don't know if we tried to swim away or whether we stepped over Pedro and escaped to the south." He waited. "Will you do that for us?"

"What if he asks me why I stayed?"

"Tell him that you are a coward—that you prefer safety over freedom."

"But—"

"Point to Pedro and tell Alazar that he was guarding us, and that if anybody is to be punished for our escape, it should be Pedro." Joshua was getting angry and ready to strike the young man. "Choose now—to die as a slave or to live as a free man."

It took a moment, but Tyler nodded. "I will come with you, Joshua." The other five agreed also.

Within ten minutes, the eight men had boarded the boat and rowed out to sea and east along the shore.

"Hey!" It was Barker—the other teenager. "Look what I found under the front deck!" He reached past a water cask and pulled out two canvas bags. "Whoever this boat belonged to, they left some of their things for us."

"What is it?"

He looked into the lighter bag. "This one is full of dried meat and some sort of fruit." He dumped the heavier bag into the bottom of the boat. "Three knives, one hand ax, a coil of what looks like horse tail hair, and several candles." He looked up at Joshua. "This is good, isn't it?"

"Yes—very good." Joshua pointed at the cask. "Is there anything in that cask?"

Simbatu pulled it free and opened the bung. "It's water, but most of it is gone."

"We are free from our slavery, but we need food and water." Joshua pointed at the cask. "A man can live for several days without food, but in this climate, he will die in two days without water."

Simbatu set the cask down. "Then we need to stop at the first stream we see and fill this to the top."

"He's right, and where there's fresh water, there are trees and plants." Joshua picked up the coil of horse hair. "I know how to make snares, and with the ax and knives, I can make a bow and arrows for larger game."

Tyler held up his hand. "Where are we going, Joshua?"

"I don't know yet—away from Cuba and slavery."

"Joshua." It was Barker. "I was a seaman aboard the *Harvester*—one of His Majesty's men of war. I know the windward passage." He pointed past the eastern tip of Cuba. "Hispaniola is our only choice."

"Why?"

"Because Jamaica is too far, and several of us have British warrants on our heads."

Joshua turned to Tyler. "We're going to Hispaniola."

"Joshua." It was Barker again. "The Yumuri River is ten or twelve miles ahead. There is a village with several hundred people and a convent. We can fill our water cask in the river and with any luck, we can get food from the nuns."

"What if Alazar has sent riders to them?"

"No." Joshua turned to Tyler. "The guard he left to watch over us is probably waking about now. It will be some time before Alazar discovers that we are gone, and then with any luck, they will follow our footprints and only search to the west."

☠ ☠ ☠

Saint Helena's Catholic Church stood on the eastern shore of the Yumuri River. Several nuns were just coming from the building as Joshua and Simbatu walked onto the grounds carrying the empty cask. They stopped a hundred feet away and called. "Good morning!"

The nuns looked about at the two strange men, stopped, and called back. "Good morning! May we help you?"

"Simbatu." Joshua turned and whispered. "Our story is that we were taken by pirates and set adrift in one of the ship's boats, and we're trying to get across the windward passage to Hispaniola and the bay of Saint Nicolas to rejoin our crew."

"I may not agree with the religion of Rome, but lying is still lying." He shook his head. "I will not lie to get their help."

"What?" Joshua set down the cask and faced his friend. "You honestly believe that we will earn more sympathy and receive better treatment from these nuns by telling them that we are eight escaped slaves from Baracoa?"

"It's the truth, Joshua. That's what we are and that's what we did."

"It's the truth that could get us hunted down, arrested, and hung." He gave a frustrated huff. "You keep telling me how your God is helping us. If that is true, that he sent those two thieves to be caught and executed so that we could have their boat, would he now want to see us hanging from ropes after he got us this far?"

"You can't lie to those women, Joshua."

"Enough!" Joshua picked up the water cask, took several steps toward the women, and called. "Hello! We are survivors of a pirate raid on our ship. We were put to sea in one of the ship's boats and just now reached this place. We are trying to get to the Bay Saint Nicolas where our captain and the rest of our crew said to meet them. We need water and food for the voyage. Do you know how far away that place is? "

"Food and water—yes—we have food and water." The older of the two looked past the two. "Is it just the two of you?"

"No. There are six others." Joshua pointed. "They are waiting down by our boat."

"Eight of you." The younger nun turned and spoke to the older one. "That's a one-day trip if they have a sail and good winds."

"Just food and water—enough to make the passage." He raised the water cask. "We mostly need water."

"I'm sure we have several empty casks you could have." The older nun looked toward the river. "Go get the others. We will tend to your physical needs first, and then see about the provisions you will need."

"We are able-bodied men and will work for our food." Joshua walked toward the two and noticed that one of the hinges on the door was broken. "None of us have our tools with us, but while we are here, we can provide our labor if anything needs repair."

"Yes." The older nun gave a smile. "We have several broken things that we have been asking the Lord about." As the other six stepped close, she turned to Joshua and Simbatu. "You two are wearing seaman's breaches and shirts, but these others are wearing slave clothes, they smell of sugar, and those cuts on their hands and forearms tell another story."

"We're…"

"You're escaped slaves, aren't you?"

"Yes." Simbatu looked to Joshua and back to the older nun. "My friend doesn't believe either of us has a soul, and he was afraid that the truth would get us hanged."

"My name is Sister Margaret." She turned to the younger woman. "This is Sister Alice." She looked at Joshua. "We hate slavery and we don't turn in runaway slaves." She spread her arms. "Welcome to Saint Helena's Catholic Church."

The eight men stayed at the convent for two days—enough time to repair two doors, replace several broken tiles in the sanctuary, and build a new wall around the well. By the early morning of the third day, the eight were back at sea with a compass, the food, three water casks, and a letter to the nuns at Saint Nicolas Convent.

CHAPTER FIVE:
The Buccaneers

Joshua and the other seven sailed along the northern coast of Hispaniola until they came to the first large river. They lowered and stowed their sail and took turns rowing their boat up the slow-moving current of the Los Trois River, keeping watch for a place to make camp go ashore and camp. The sun was nearing the western horizon when they finally beached the boat on a sand bar.

"It's late. We will rest and spend the night here."

"What then, Joshua?"

"I don't know, Simbatu. Some sort of plan." Joshua pointed to the trees. "For now, our greatest needs are food and protection from harm."

"What kind of plan?" It was Tyler. "We don't know where we are. We only have these limited tools, and Nature is indifferent to our plight."

"Find yourself a place to sleep, Tyler. We will talk about this in the morning."

As the two gathered leaves and grass to make themselves beds, Simbatu gave Joshua a gentle poke to the chest. "Look at what God has done for us, Joshua. He had Alazar send us to that beach, then He led you to that boat, then He led us to that convent where he gave us food and water, and now we are long gone from Cuba, the hatred of Alazar, and that life of slavery."

"Is that how your God works?"

"Well, look at us."

"Yes—look at us. First, your God killed all those men with cholera to set eight other men free?"

"How can you not believe that God did this?" Simbatu shook his head. "If you don't believe in God, then what do you believe in?"

"I believe in myself, because only a cruel and heartless God would do such things!"

"I'm right next to you, Joshua. I have seen the same cruelty you have. How is it that you are rejecting this salvation while I am thanking my Lord for it?"

"Because you are an ignorant and gullible fool, and I am not."

"No, my friend. God called to me and my soul heard him."

"Well, my soul hasn't heard that call."

"There! You just admitted it!"

"What?"

"You just admitted that you have a soul!" He gave a laugh. "The only problem with your soul is that it wasn't listening."

"Well…" Joshua thought for a long moment. "Okay. I'll give you this much. If a black man has a soul, then maybe a white man does too."

"Do you know why your soul matters to God?"

"I know what my mother and Becky told me—that after we die, our soul lives forever with God in heaven or separated from God in hell."

"They were right." Simbatu arranged the last of the leaves, laid down, and looked up into the evening sky. "She's right about everything she told you."

"Can we talk about something else?"

"Certainly, but if you're not right with God yet—believing who Jesus is and what he did for you on the cross—this is the most important thing to talk about until you do believe in him."

"Well, the way he's treated me so far, I don't much care if I'm right or wrong with him."

"How can you blame God for the evil that men have done to you?"

"God may not have done this to me directly, but it makes no sense that he would stand by and allow the Mohammedans, the Spaniards, that factor at the plantation, and that ship's captain to do what they did to me."

"When you were in that chain locker on the *Crow* you must have prayed to God."

"Of course, I prayed. Every man prays when he is facing certain death."

"What did you pray for?"

"That he would allow me to escape so that I might find and marry Rebecca Keyes."

"Is that all?"

"I prayed for revenge—to find and kill Michael and Edwin Drake—and to kill that Savannah constable, Damon Hobson."

"Look where we are, Joshua. We are free men. God has answered those first prayers, and in so doing, he freed me and these other six men with you."

It took Joshua a long moment to consider Simbatu's words. "Maybe your god is real, but I don't think I will ever understand him."

"Can a toddler understand his father or his mother?"

"No, but…" Joshua laid down. "Enough. Can we talk about this tomorrow?"

"Yes." Simbatu turned away, and within minutes the two were fast asleep.

☠ ☠ ☠

Early the next morning, Joshua awoke to a rough kick to his hip. "Ah!" He sat up and looked up at the man silhouetted against the dawn. "Why did you kick me?"

"Ha! You didn't think we'd find you!"

"Who are you?" He could now make out that there were four of them, and they all held pistols. "What do you want?"

"You didn't think we saw you drop your sail and row up the river, did you?"

"Oh, no!" He looked across at the other seven who were still sleeping. "How did you find us so quickly?"

"So quickly?" It was the tallest of the group. "You Spanish mercenaries came looking for us in broad daylight. How could you think that we would not see you?"

"We—"

"Hey!" Simbatu turned over. "What's all the talking, Joshua?" He looked up at the men. "Who are they?"

"Enough!" The tall man gave Joshua another kick to the hip. "On your feet!"

As ordered, Joshua pushed himself up and rubbed his sore hip. "What are your orders? Does Alazar want us killed here, or does he want us taken back to Cuba?"

"Who is Alazar, and why would you think that…?" The man looked to the others and back to Joshua. "Ah!" He gave a laugh. "You eight are runaway sugar slaves, and that means the Spaniards didn't send you here to kill us."

"How could we kill you?" Joshua spread his arms. "Look at us. We have no pistols or rifles—only three knives and a hand ax." He pointed at the boat. "That boat and what's in it is all we have."

"Ha!" The tall man offered his hand. "My name is Alan. I am the leader of what's left of our clan of buccaneers."

"My name is Joshua Smoot, and this is my closest friend, Simbatu." He took the offered hand. "He is convinced that God did this for us."

"Amazing." Alan turned to the man next to him. "They are like us—hunted men who just want to be free."

"Pardon my ignorance, but what is a buccaneer?"

"We are hunters who dry the meat of cattle and goats in buccans, and then we trade it to passing ships for the things the forest does not provide."

"Is that what you were doing—hunting cattle to shoot—when you found us?"

"We used to shoot and butcher them where we found them, but now we rope them and make them walk back to our camp. Once they are there, we kill them, cut their flesh into strips, and then we preserve it in smoke-filled tents called a buccans."

"Did you do something wrong that made the Spaniards come after you?"

"No. The Spaniards have always been our best customers."

"That makes no sense, Alan. If the Spaniards trade for the meat, then why would they turn on you like that?"

"Because every two or three years, the King of Spain issues a decree that whoever kills his cattle on Hispaniola is his enemy and must be hunted down and executed."

"We are free men, but we don't know what to do or where to go. Until we know, can we join your clan?" Joshua pointed to his other men. "We are hard workers. We are willing to trade our sweat for a place to live and eat."

"Then we welcome you." Alan pointed into the forest. "Follow us."

An hour later, Alan and his three hunters led Joshua and his seven back toward the coast into a canyon near the river mouth. Four men who were working at the tables stopped and watched the twelve men enter the canyon. "We chose this spot because the meat cures better after being soaked in sea water, and we're close to where the ships anchor."

Simbatu walked toward the tables, turned, and put a hand to his nose. "What is that smell?"

"Look down. You're walking on it."

The Ethiopian looked down at the red soil. "Is that what I think it is?"

"We call this Blood Canyon, because this is where we bring the cattle and goats to be slaughtered, skinned, and where we cut the meat from the bones into strips." He pointed up the canyon. "The smoking tents—the buccans—are further up the canyon just this side of our camp."

"Show us what we must do."

"Those four will show you how to cut the meat from those two carcasses into strips the thickness of a finger, remove the fat, and put it into those sleds. When the sleds are full, pull them up the canyon to the buccans. Then come back and wait for us."

It was bloody work, but the time went quickly. By noon, all the meat was cut from the bones and moved to the smoke tents. The eight returned to the slaughter tables where Alan was waiting with several more of his men and a bellowing cow.

"Once we kill this animal and you finish cutting her into strips, we'll show you how we fill the buccans and set the fires. That will be your next job while we trap and bring back more of the King's cattle.

By dusk, the new kill was bled, skinned, gutted, and cut in strips. The next day, all four buccans were fired up and filled with the meat.

"How long does the drying take?"

"This time of year, two days at the most. During the monsoons when the air is wetter, it will take another day." Alan took one of the dried strips from one of the bags and handed it to Joshua. "We smoke it until there is no give when pinched."

"How long will the dried meat last?"

"Forever, as long as it's kept dry." Alan took back the meat and tore it in half. "Here. Try it."

"Umm." Joshua closed his teeth on the leathery meat. "So, this is what we were fed on the ships."

"On board the ships, the cooks soak the dried and salted meat in water for several hours until it softens."

☠ ☠ ☠

Time passed quickly. Within two years, Joshua and Simbatu were leading their own hunters out to trap the wild cattle. Then during the early months of their third year as buccaneers, the Spanish King issued another decree to his military, bringing several ships to Hispaniola to hunt down and kill the poachers of his cattle.

"To the boats! To the boats!"

"What's happening, Alan?"

"The King has declared us poachers again. We must flee before they get here."

"Where can we go?"

"To Tortuga!"

CHAPTER SIX:
Tortuga and El Pescador

*T*he pickpockets of England reasoned that if a man's neck could be stretched for a farthing, it might as well stretch for a whole purse full of gold. Driven to crime by starvation or the abuses of the law, many in the Caribbean likewise figured they might as well take a whole ship as a man's purse. Thusly, new names were added to "the account" of the Brotherhood of the Coast every day. In the 1600s, for the pirates of French and English extraction, the small island of Tortuga suited this new trade well. Not only were its hills abundant with streams, fruit, and game, it was situated at the eastern gate of the most heavily traveled waterway between the Spanish Main and Europe, the Windward Passage.

Warehouses to store the pirate's swag and taverns to fulfill the lusts of their hearts sprang up on Tortuga like weeds. But now, in mid-June 1764, as Joshua Smoot led his fellow buccaneers toward its southern coast, past Devil's Rock, and into what was commonly called Pirate's Cove, there remained only the memory of this once-busy haven of rest. The thriving commerce of piracy had been replaced by fishing boats and families spawned by the pirates and prostitutes.

The arrival of the two boats on the south shore of Tortuga was noted by the red-headed youth, Henry Morgan. "Finally! The buccaneers have finally come to Tortuga!" He jumped down from the roof of the Musket's Muzzle, ran across the beach, and waded out into the water to meet the first boat. "Welcome to Tortuga! My name is Henry Morgan!"

"I'm glad to meet you, Henry Morgan. I'm Joshua Smoot." Joshua jumped into the shallow water, turned, and called back to the following boats. "Listen up! When you get to shore, pull your boat out and bring your things over to me!"

"Are you a pirate, Joshua?"

"No—just one among a clan of buccaneers…" He paused, not sure what he should tell the lad.

"I know what buccaneers do, an' since there be no cattle on Tortuga, that means yer here fer somethin' else besides hunting."

"Who are you, Henry Morgan?"

"I'm nobody and I'm everybody." He spread his arms and turned around. "If you need something, I can get it for you." By now, the rest of the men had beached their boats and assembled around the two. Henry looked at the twenty men. "What do you buccaneers need?"

"I'll tell you, Henry, but if you betray us, I swear by John Flint's black heart that I'll come back and do to you what we do to the King's cattle."

"I may be an orphan, and I may be poor, but I'm no back-stabbing mutineer that rats out his own future."

"Okay." Joshua turned to Alan and got a nod. "Every few years, the King of Spain decrees that all buccaneers—the men who poach his cattle—be driven off his land or killed."

"Then you have no choice but to take your two boats back to sea and capture the first ship you find." Henry held up his mangrove root. "When you do that, take me with you."

"Well, since you put it that way, I guess we are pirates."

"Every pirate captain needs a cabin boy, and I'm the one to fill that billet."

"Ha!" Joshua looked to the others. "I'll tell you what, Henry Morgan. If that is what we do, and I ever get me a real pirate ship, I'll come back here to Tortuga and make you a member of my crew."

"No! Those are just words!" Henry pulled his knife and drove the point into the middle of his right palm. "Make it a blood oath, Cap'n." He handed Joshua the knife. "Cut yerself and repeat those words so everybody hears ya."

"I…" Joshua looked to the others and got smiles and nods. "Very well." He cut his palm and took Henry's hand. "If I become a pirate someday, I swear by John Flint's black heart that I'll come back for you, Henry Morgan."

Henry held up his bloody hand to the others. "You all heard him!"

"Enough!" Joshua pointed inland. "The Spaniards may come here looking for us. Do you know of a place on Tortuga where we can hide until they tire of the search so that we can return to Hispaniola?"

"Yes." He pointed north at the canyons. "Follow that stream up the canyon until it reaches the spring—the place where the water comes up out of the ground. Then turn to the east through the forest until you come to a meadow with a large tree in the center with a tree house among its branches—my tree house. You will be safe there." He turned and pointed at the boats. "But first, you will need to hide your boats. If the Spaniards search the coast for your landing, it will be those two boats that betray you."

Joshua looked east and west along the beach. "There." He pointed at the string of fishing boats. "We can hide them among those other boats."

"And then I can lead you up to my tree house."

"No!" Joshua held up his bloody hand. "Our blood oath made you my crewman and me your captain. That means you have to follow my orders."

"What is your order, Cap'n Smoot?"

"I want you to stay here in case the Spaniards come."

"And if they do?"

"Then come to your tree house and tell us."

"And what if they never come?"

"If we don't hear from you in a week, we'll come back down and make a new plan."

The lad took the buccaneers to the base of the canyon, held up his bloody hand and backed away. "Make sure you turn east at the spring, through the trees for a furlong, and then out into my meadow!"

With Joshua and Simbatu in the lead, it took them just under two hours to scale the mountain and reach the meadow. Joshua put up a hand. "Stay here. I'll go out and make sure it's safe." A moment later, after climbing up into Henry's tree house, Joshua waved the others to the tree.

"This is good." Alan leaned his rifle against the tree and looked around. "We have enough food in our packs for several weeks, and with that spring, all the fresh water we need."

"What about a fire?" It was Grady—one of the newer members of the clan. "Should we gather some wood?"

"No." Alan shook his head. "The Spaniards will see the smoke."

"How long will we stay here, Joshua?"

"Alan and I will go down in a week to meet with Henry. Hopefully, the Spaniards will have given up their search by then."

"And then we return to our buccans at Hispaniola?"

"Yes."

The next morning, the clan was awakened by screams. "The Spaniards! The Spaniards are coming!" Henry ran out onto the meadow, stopped, turned about, and pointed. "Take up your rifles and run back into the forest!"

Joshua ran across to the lad. "How many ships?"

"Just one, but there are a lot of soldiers—forty or fifty." He pointed. "They'll be here in half a glass."

"How did they find us?"

"When you came ashore, there were two fishermen mending their nets. They must have heard me telling you about this meadow and my tree house."

Alan called out to the clan. "Everybody! The Spaniards will be here shortly. Take up your arms and packs and follow me!" He started toward the north. "We must leave this place before they get here!"

"No!" Henry ran to Alan, grabbed his arm, and pointed. "Once you leave this forest, there is only open country with no place to hide! Your only chance is to stay in the forest until they give up the search."

"Henry's right, Alan. We wouldn't stand a chance in the open."

Joshua turned about at Henry. "How did they find us?"

"It was two of the fishermen. They must have heard us talking on the beach."

"Damn them!" Joshua looked at the forest. "If we hide, they'll search until they find us." He held up his rifle. "We need to set up an ambush along the tree line and take down as many as we can."

Within minutes, the twenty buccaneers gathered up their belongings and were hunkered down to either side of the trail along the tree line. While they prepared, Henry ran back down the hill to watch.

"They're here, Cap'n!"

"Listen up!" Joshua stood and called to the others. "We'll have one shot with each rifle and pistol! We must kill as many of them as we can in that first volley, and then we need to scatter to the forest!"

"They'll come after us, Joshua!"

"I know, so we must be ready to fight with our cutlasses and knives." He shook his head. "We have no other choice."

As Henry predicted, the soldiers could be heard coming up the trail. One of them called out. "Alto!" There were some more orders given in Spanish, and then a single soldier walked out into the meadow a dozen steps, pointed at the tree house, and called back. There was more calling back and forth, and then the soldier continued to the tree house and climbed the ladder. He called back again.

"This isn't going to work, Joshua."

"I know." Joshua looked to the others and whispered. "Pass the word to fall back into the woods and meet together at the spring."

As the last two buccaneers were backing away from their places of ambush, one of the Spaniards saw the movement, turned, and fired his rifle. "Amboscada! Amboscada!" The battle lasted only minutes and turned quickly from firearms to cutlasses and pikes. Out of the smoke came screams and confusion in both English and Spanish. When the smoke finally cleared, five buccaneers lay dead among the trees, along with ten of the Spaniards.

It took a half glass before the last two surviving buccaneers found their way to the spring.

"We've lost eight men, Joshua."

"They may not all be dead Alan but simply haven't found their way back to us yet."

"Cap'n Smoot!" Henry ran up to the two and pointed back toward the meadow. "They've got three of your men on their knees under the tree house, and their leader is calling to you in English." Joshua and Alan followed Henry back through the trees to a place of seclusion. The lad called out. "We're here for a parley! Tell us again what you said before!"

"I knew you could hear me!" The Spanish officer searched the forest while he spoke. "I am a reasonable man! If the rest of you will surrender your weapons and give yourselves up, we promise that you will be taken back to Spain for a fair trial!" When he got no reply, he called again. "The afternoon is upon us, and it will soon be dark. If you do not surrender yourselves before the shadow of the forest reaches across the meadow to the tree house, these three men will be tried, convicted, and executed as you watch!"

"What do we do, Joshua?"

"The Spaniards are here by the King's decree to kill every buccaneer on Hispaniola and they outnumber us by more than double. Those three men are already dead, and we cannot risk any more lives to save them."

"They came on a ship with eight guns, Cap'n Smoot. She's named *El Pescador*, an' she'd make a fine pirate ship if you and the others would sneak aboard an' take her."

"Did you see how many men they left aboard?"

"I only saw two topside, but there might be more than that below deck."

"We have an hour before the shadow reaches your tree house." Joshua looked across the meadow. "We must act or die like those three." He turned to Henry. "If we follow you, could you get us down through the canyon to the beach before dark?"

"Aye, Cap'n."

Joshua stood and shouted to the Spaniard. "I must talk to the others! We will tell you our decision before the shadow reaches the tree!"

"I will wait for your answer!"

"Let's go back to the others." A moment later, Joshua jumped up onto a rock next to the spring. "Henry is going to lead us down to the coast where the Spaniards have left their ship. We will hide until it is dark, and then we will row out and take their ship."

"Damn right!" Alan pointed out at the meadow. "Those Spaniards killed five of us already, and they will kill those three shortly. Whoever is on board their ship must die like them."

"Not until we know who those men are."

"They're Spaniards, Joshua! They are here to kill buccaneers!"

"They might be Englishmen who were impressed into service against their will." Joshua looked around at the eleven. "Have any of you ever crewed on a ship?" One-by-one, the men shook their heads. "We could surely use their sailing skills."

"What?" It was Alan. "You're going to give them that choice—to die or join us?"

"Yes."

"And if the Spaniards had you on your knees in that meadow with the shadow of death inching toward you, and they gave you the same choice—to join them or die—would you choose death?"

"I know what you're saying, Alan." He looked to Simbatu. "I believe that men should be given the chance to repent of the course they are on, and choose another course, regardless of who they are."

"Well, since we are going to be at sea, and since you're going to be our captain, if they choose to join us and it causes trouble, that trouble will be on you."

"A question, Joshua." It was one of the newer men. "Once we take the ship, what then?"

"We'll sail away to the open sea and freedom."

"We are buccaneers." Alan spread his arms. "We know nothing about the sea or how to sail a ship."

"That's why we must give those men a choice." Joshua pointed to the meadow. "It's time for each of you to make your choice to follow me as your captain, or walk across that meadow and surrender yourselves to the Spanish soldiers."

"If we can do what you've said—take their ship and sail away—what then?"

"We sail to Florida and then turn north along the coast."

Tyler turned to Henry. "When do we stop being buccaneers and start being pirates?"

"When you take your first prize and split the booty—that's when."

"Henry's right. There is a fleet of small cargo ships called coasters. They carry no guns and are easy pickings."

"How far north will we go?"

"We'll make port at Charles Town."

"What's in Charles Town?"

"Rebecca Keyes—my betrothed."

"And if you find her, then what?"

"Then *El Pescador* will be yours to do with as you please."

"What about me, Joshua?" It was Henry. "We have a blood covenant. You aren't leaving me here to face the Spaniards by myself, are you?"

"You're of no value to them, Henry, and we twelve may be killed tonight."

"But—"

"You have my blood oath that if I can't find Rebecca, I will return for you."

Henry looked at the wound on his palm and up at Joshua. "I will be right here waiting for you, Cap'n Smoot."

☠ ☠ ☠

When the twelve reached the beach, the two fishermen were waiting for them. "Sirs! We have a confession!"

"Are you the two who told the Spaniards where to find us?"

"Yes but…"

Joshua pulled a pistol from his sash. "On your knees traitors!"

"Please!" The older of the two pointed to the village. "We have families."

"You caused the deaths of eight of us. For that, you will give your lives as retribution."

"They said they would pay us to tell them where you went, but when we refused, they threatened to torture and kill us." The man clasped his hands together. "Have mercy on us, good sir!"

"Joshua." It was Simbatu. "These are not the killers of our men. They had no choice."

"I know you're right but…" Joshua turned and looked out to the Spanish ship and back to canyon. "The Spaniards will be down the hill soon, and the sun just set." Joshua lowered the hammer on his pistol. "Get the boats down to the shore. Once it's dark, we go."

An hour later, the twelve buccaneers climbed silently up the sides of the small ship—six men to port and six to starboard. At Joshua's signal, the buccaneers swarmed over the gunwales.

While Joshua and Simbatu led their four below, Alan and his five killed the two sailors topside and threw their bodies overboard. When Joshua and his five came back topside, he looked about for the sailors.

"Where are they?"

"They were Spanish and they fought us." He pointed. "We fed them to the sharks,"

"Very well." Joshua stepped in front of the eleven. "The ship is well-stocked with food, clothes, and it carries eight guns." He pointed forward. "With no winds, we'll need to row our way to the open sea."

"How do we do that, Joshua?"

"There are eight sweeps stowed in the overhead on the gun deck. When the anchor is raised, eight of you will man those sweeps to get us away from this place."

Alan stood. "Show us what to do, and we'll do it."

It took only ten minutes for the anchor to pull loose from the bottom and for the eight to pull *El Pescador* away to the west toward the Windward Passage.

As the sun was rising, a gentle breeze began blowing across the ship from the stern. Joshua stepped down the ladder to the gun deck. "You can put away those sweeps, come topside, and help raise the sails."

"Thank you." Once the sweeps were stowed, Alan led the men topside and looked up at the rigging. "We taught you to kill cattle, Joshua. Now it's your turn to teach us to sail a ship."

"Aye." Joshua looked at the main mast and chose the lowest sail. "Wait here and watch everything I do." In a moment, he was up the port shrouds to the mast and then side-stepped his way across the foot ropes, untying the buntlines as he went. He called down. "These small ropes that I'm untying are called buntlines! This long piece of wood that the sail is attached to is called the yard." With the main sail free, Joshua returned to the deck and stepped to the taffrail. "These ropes are attached to that yard and the sail through a system of pulleys in a way that we can raise and lower the yard and open or close the sail." He pointed to other ropes. "These ropes allow us to turn the sail to catch the wind, and that capture drives the ship forward."

"If you tell us which ones to pull or release, Captain, we'll do it."

"I have an idea." Ten minutes later, Joshua was back with a pair of shears, several pieces of gaily colored cloth, and one of the Spanish uniforms." As the men watched, he cut the cloth into strips and then tied them to the various ropes. "There. When I want you to raise the yard, I'll tell you the name of the rope and the color tied to it. When I want the yard rotated to catch the wind, I'll tell you another color." He looked around at the men. "Does that help?"

"Yes, Captain." Alan looked around at the others. "That's unless any of you don't know your colors."

For the next twenty minutes, all the buccaneers pulled and released the hemp ropes as Joshua commanded. Once they had raised and lowered the main sheet several times, Joshua gathered them on the main deck below the quarterdeck.

"Is it starting to make sense?"

Aye!" Alan nodded as he brushed the hemp fibers from his hands and arms. "Tell us more about the coasters."

"The easiest prey is the fleet of small ships that move cargoes through shallow waters from town to town." He gave them an assuring nod. "Like I said, none of them carry guns or many men." Joshua pointed north. "We start where we reach the Florida coast and work our way north to Charles Town, taking whatever we want as we go."

"Is that where we'll sell what we take?"

"Yes."

"And what about the money from the cargo that we sell? How is that to be divided?"

"An even share for every man."

Alan stepped forward and pointed to the main mast. "Now that we know how to set that lowest sail, can we try to set the one above it?"

"Do I need to tie the colored cloth to the ropes?"

"No." Alan looked to the others and got an assuring nod from all but two. "Let us try it without."

"Very well." Joshua looked at the various sails and pointed. "We're running on the main sheet. That one above it is called the main gallant, and the one above that is the main royal. See if you can set it and trim the main gallant without me telling you how."

Alan turned to his mates. "You heard the captain! Let's get to it!"

"Hey!" Simbatu pointed ahead. "That ship! Is that one of your coasters, Joshua?"

Joshua stepped to the rail and shaded his eyes. "That's a sloop—a pleasure yacht. The owner has money, but the only things aboard will be their clothes, the food and drink they need, and a skeleton crew." He took the telescope from the binnacle and stepped back to the rail. "Besides, we're doing about four knots, and from their wake, I'd say they're doing twice our speed."

"But we have six cannons. Wouldn't they—"

"Look at that, Simbatu." Joshua pointed up at the main gallant—how it was sagging first one way and then the other. "Even if that was a coaster, and it carried a king's ransom in treasure, we would make fools of ourselves trying to catch and board her."

"But there will be others, right?" The Ethiopian looked at the yacht as it sped past. "We'll take at least one coaster before we reach Charles Town, right? The men will need money to spend in that place?"

"Yes—I promise."

"What's so interesting, Joshua?"

"She's the *Liberty*, and there's a woman on board watching us."

"Is she pretty?"

"I can't tell. She has the telescope to her face and looking at us." He lowered the spyglass and closed it. "They're beyond our grasp, so it doesn't matter what she looks like."

After two more days of training, the top watch spotted the first coaster. "On deck! There's a small ship ahead and to the left! If we turn a little, we should be able to cut her off!"

Joshua gave Simbatu a frustrated scowl. "They can finally handle the sails, but they don't know the talk."

"Does it matter, Joshua?"

"Not really." He looked to port and down at the compass. "Come port twenty degrees, Simbatu." Joshua called forward. "Alan! Have the gun crew ready two cannons! We'll be putting one across that ship's bow in about twelve minutes!"

"Aye!" *El Pescador* came alive. The sails were trimmed for the new course and the cannons were loaded. As ordered, a single shot was fired across the bow of the approaching ship.

To Joshua's surprise, the merchant ship dumped their sails and turned into the wind to stop dead in the water. "Alan! Dump our sails and ready the boat!"

"Who do you want with you, Captain?"

"You and two others, and you're to be armed."

The crossing took only minutes, and when Joshua and his three men jumped over the rail and down onto the deck, the captain and his crew of six were standing in ranks.

"I am Captain Joshua Smoot, and these are just three of my forty men. We are taking your cargo."

"I know how you pirates do this. You put me and my men safely aboard one of the ship's boats and set us free while you take the ship and its cargo to a port where you will sell it."

"Has this happened to you before?"

"Three times this year, sir."

"And what happened those three times?"

"The same thing as always. I report the theft to the owner of our fleet. He notifies Lloyd's of London. They give the owner the money to buy the ship back. My crew and I come back aboard, and we resume our coastal runs."

"So, the ship is insured?"

"Yes, and the cargo also."

"What is your cargo?"

"Here." The captain held out the manifest. "A dozen sheep, six pigs, and sixty baby chicks." He looked at the list. "We also carry various household goods, fifty sacks of wheat flour from the grist mill at Charles Town, shoes and clothing for both men and women, several dozen bolts of textiles from England—"

"Enough." Joshua looked at Simbatu, gave a grimace, and got a shrug in return. "You must have money aboard. How much?"

"Why?"

Joshua put his hand on his pistol. "Show me your strong box."

"Very well." The man turned and walked to the companionway that led to his cabin. "What do you intend, Captain Snort?"

"My name is Joshua Smoot, and I intend to take your money."

"Sorry." Once in his cabin, the man pushed his key into the strong box and raised the lid. There were three bags of coins inside, and a stack of British paper money. He turned. "You're not taking the *Muskrat* and our cargo?"

"Not this time."

"Uh, before you take the money, can I ask a favor?"

"What?"

"This." The man took a piece of parchment from his desk and wrote quickly. When he was finished, he handed Joshua the quill. "Can you write your name?"

"I'm not literate."

"Then sign your name to verify the amount of money you're taking from me."

"Will Lloyd's cover the theft of your money also?"

"It's called insurance, Captain Smoot. With so many pirates and privateers working these waters, every coaster is heavily insured."

"What is a privateer?"

"You…" The man gave a laugh. "You must be new at this—at piracy."

"Tell me."

"Each colony has a governor. Those governors can grant what is called a letter of marque that authorizes private sea captains to do what you are doing without fear of the gallows."

"A license to steal." Joshua dipped the quill in the ink but hesitated. He hefted the bags of silver and spread out the paper money. "You say that I'm taking eight hundred pounds sterling from you?"

"I've exaggerated the number a little."

"So, you have a pirate's heart too."

"Take the money and go, Captain Smoot, and we both walk away from this a little richer."

"Aye, and you've taught me an important lesson." With the strong box under his arm, Joshua returned to the deck where the other three were waiting. "I've decided to leave this ship and its cargo for another day." He patted the strong box with his free hand. "But, thanks to Lloyd's of London, we go away with a much better prize than I anticipated."

CHAPTER SEVEN:
Rebecca is Sold

*L*ife was good at the Fayssoux estate. The days, weeks, and months passed by quickly, and Rebecca had become a part of the family. Likewise, after more than two years of shopping for the family, she was a regular at the market. As she moved from one merchant to the next, each had their special way of welcoming her. Tully—the old Negro woman would hold up one of her woven grass hats while she told a quick story and offered a gem of knowledge. Martin, the blacksmith, wanted to know everything about Mary and her little boy. After buying everything on her list, she would push her cart to East Bay Street where Samuel Paine maintained a lively business selling live fish.

Rebecca knew that no matter what she bought, the cook would always object to at least one item on the cart—that she had spent too much money for fresh beets or that she did not buy enough of something else. Their bickering had long ago turned into a shopping day game between the two. The meals that Margie and Becky prepared for the family were consistently of the highest quality and the two always received praise from Lady Fayssoux.

One morning while Rebecca made ready to walk to the market, she approached the housekeeper. "Do you have a moment, Susan?"

"Of course, Becky. What is it?"

"I have a serious question—something I probably know the answer to before I ask it."

"Umm." Susan gave a smile. "Does this have something to do with Samuel Paine, the famous Fishmonger of Bay Street?"

"So, you've noticed."

"Everybody's noticed how a lowly fishmonger at the market grew his living fish business into what it is today, and how you and he have become close."

"Yes—Sam's doing quite well."

"How many captains are bringing him live fish now that he has his shop?"

"Last I heard, there were three."

"Sorry, Becky. I got sidetracked there. You had a question?"

"Yes." Rebecca took a large breath and exhaled slowly. "His wife died last year, leaving him with two small children. He has asked me for my hand in marriage."

"Umm." She wrinkled her nose, which always meant she did not like something. "That's going to be a problem."

"I know but—"

"If you and Joshua had come to us already married, that would have been acceptable."

"But you and Grady got married two years ago—just a few months after Mary and I arrived."

"He and I came here separately, but since we both work in the same household, Doctor and Lady Fayssoux allowed it."

"So..?" Rebecca bit her lip. "Is it because Sam is free and I am still obligated for another four and a half years into my seven years?"

"If you married Samuel Paine, he would want you to live with him so you could be a proper mother to his children. That would violate your obligation to Doctor Fayssoux."

"What if I promised to only be gone on my day off?"

"What kind of a wife and mother would you be for only one day a week?"

"He needs a wife."

"But you do not need a husband?" Susan shook her head. "I can tell you without hesitation that the doctor and his wife will not allow it."

"But..."

"I understood that you were waiting for Joshua to return. Have you already given up on him?"

"No but..." Rebecca closed her eyes and gave a sigh. "So, I best tell him so he can begin looking elsewhere."

"Yes, as hard as that will be, Becky." Susan gave a grimace and a nod. "Since you're headed for the market, you should go to his shop on your way."

It took Rebecca fifteen minutes to reach East Bay Street. There were a dozen people—mostly women—waiting outside in a queue. Rebecca excused herself and walked to the front of the line.

"Becky!" Samuel reached into one of the ponds and pulled up a large grouper and called. "I've been holding this one for you!"

"I'm on my way to the market. I'll come back for the fish on my way home." She looked around at the other people. "I have to talk to you in private."

"In private?" He gave her a worried look. "That doesn't sound very good."

"Please." She pointed to the back room. "It's not good."

He dropped the grouper and turned to one of his helpers. "Take over here for a few minutes."

"Sure." The boy turned to the next person in line as Samuel followed Rebecca. Once alone, he turned and gave her a light kiss. "Is it what we feared?"

"I'm so sorry, Sam."

"Yeah…" He looked down at the floor for a long moment.

"They have rules. There's just so much that—"

"What if I bought your remaining years?"

"You would do that?" She corrected herself. "You have enough money to do that?"

"I don't know." He looked about the room as if the answer was on one of the walls. "The doctor paid a price for you—several hundred dollars. If we knew what your remaining years are worth to him, then I could save up, buy your freedom, and then we could be married."

"I'll ask Doctor Fayssoux, but he might not want to let me go."

"Why not?"

"They depend on me for a lot of things. I'm just saying that—"

"It can't hurt to ask him, Becky."

"Alright." She gave him a kiss, turned, and started toward the front of the store. "I'll be back for that grouper and several more fish in an hour."

"I'll save him for you."

Rebecca walked to the market in turmoil. When she finally reached the northern building, she stopped and stood in the morning sun for several minutes. *Maybe this is best. What if I got married and then Joshua comes looking for me? What would I do then?*

She looked about at the crush of shoppers coming and going and noticed a man she had seen the day before. *That's odd. He's always nearby, yet he never buys anything.* She watched him for a moment while he pretended to study a small picture frame.

She pushed her cart past him and purposely drove to the far end of the building where she stopped and turned about. He was twenty feet away, looking at the bottom of a tea cup. *He is following me! Who is he, and what could he want?*

She looked at her list and set a course for her favorite vendors. When she finished with everything but the fish, she looked about for the man. *Good— he's not there.*

Believing that she had lost him, she left the southern building by a side door, drove up West Market Street, and north toward East Bay Street. Each hundred feet, she looked about to see if he was following. To her relief, he was not there.

Rebecca parked her cart at Samuel's fish market and stepped inside. "Sam!"

"Becky!" He wiped his hands on his waist towel and stepped from behind the tanks. "I have an idea."

"Me too." She gave him a kiss. "Give me a half hour to put away the groceries, and then come to the back gate. Doctor Fayssoux will be home for lunch and we can ask him together."

"That's what I was going to say." He returned the kiss. "See? We're perfect for each other. I'm certain the doctor will see that and agree to release you to me."

"A half hour then, and maybe put on some better clothes."

"I'll be there."

When she stepped onto the street, she made another search for the man from the market. Satisfied that she had lost him, she headed down Tradd Street and then turned into the alleyway toward the back gate. "Oh, no!" She came to an abrupt stop as the man stepped from behind a red brick wall and stood between her and the back gate of the Fayssoux estate.

"Who are you? Why are you following me?"

"I…" The man reached into his coat "I have something—"

Before he could finish, she screamed and rammed him in the legs with her cart. "No, you don't!" He went to the ground along under the cart with most of her groceries strewn about him on the bricks.

"Wait, Rebecca! My name is Jeremy Tanner! I was sent—" Before he could finish, Becky grabbed the largest grouper and hit him in the head several times.

"Stay down, Jeremy Tanner! If you follow me into the yard, Grady Olsen will shoot you!" Becky ran past him and down the alley to the back gate. She looked around for help. "Grady!" The carriage house was empty, so she pushed through the gate and called. "Margaret! I need your help!"

The cook came from the kitchen wiping her hands. "What's wrong, Becky, and where's the cart?"

"It's in the alley!" She turned and pointed. "It's spilled in the alley!"

"You're a big girl. Go back and get it!"

"You don't understand, Margaret! There's a man! He was following me at the market, and he followed me home! When I turned into the alley, he was right there, waiting for me!"

"Is he still there?"

"I don't know." Rebecca gave a quick look to the cart but couldn't see him. "I rammed him with the cart and then I hit him with one of the fish. I might have hurt him."

"Stay there! I'll be right back." The cook returned with two meat cleavers and handed one to Rebecca. "We'll take care of this masher." They marched together back to the cart.

"He's gone!"

Margie looked about. "Well, that beating with the fish must have scared him off."

"He was lying right there."

"Let's get these groceries picked up, and then we can tell Conway what happened. He'll know what to do."

The two gathered up the groceries, pushed the cart up the alley, through the back yard, and across to the kitchen door.

Conway met them at the door. "Rebecca!"

"Yes?"

"What in God's Holy name have you done, young lady?"

"I…" She looked at Margaret and pointed to the alley. "There was a man. He was following me at the market, and when I came through the alley, he was there."

"What did you do to him, Rebecca?"

"I…" She handed the cleaver to Margaret. "I pushed the cart at him, and then I hit him with one of these fish."

"Then you don't know yet."

Margaret stepped between the two. "It's just as she told you, Conway." She held up a man's pocketbook. "When we picked up the spilled groceries, we found this." She opened it. "His name is Jeremy Tanner, and he's a King's solicitor."

"Mister Tanner is upstairs with the doctor as we speak."

"Oh, Lord!" She looked at Margie and back to the butler. "Am I to be arrested because I defend myself?"

"I was told to send you up immediately when you returned."

"But look at me!" She wiped her hands on her apron. "I stink of fish." She stepped forward and held up her hands. "Smell me!"

"The doctor wants you in his study now!" He took the pocketbook, turned, and marched into the building ahead of her. "Come!"

Fearful that her master had received a formal complaint from the man in the alley, Rebecca followed the butler up the stairs to the study. As Conway stepped into the room, Rebecca peeked around the doorway. The man was in his shirtsleeves and was wiping his face with a moist towel.

"You dropped your pocketbook in the alley, sir."

"Thank you." Tanner took the pocketbook and looked inside. Satisfied, he set it on the desk next to the small picture frame.

Just then, one of the maids stepped past Rebecca with a folded coat. "We did our best, sir. Your coat has been wiped and brushed as clean as we can make it."

"Thank you, Jenny." The doctor took the coat and turned to Rebecca. "Step inside, Rebecca."

"Yes, sir."

The doctor turned to Conway. "Mister Tanner and I need a private moment with Miss Keyes."

As Conway closed the door behind him, Rebecca began to cry. "Please, Doctor Fayssoux. I can explain."

Jeremy held up a hand to the doctor and turned to Rebecca. "You don't need to explain anything, Rebecca. You were fearful of a man who was obviously following you, and only did what any young woman would do."

"I…" She pointed toward the alley. "I thought you were going to hurt me. That's why I pushed the cart into you and hit you with that fish." She looked at the doctor in fear. "Am I going to jail?"

"No, Rebecca." Jeremy put on his coat, picked up the framed picture, and slipped it into his pocket. "But you are going somewhere."

"What?" She looked to the doctor. "I don't understand."

"I say this with mixed feelings." Doctor Fayssoux gave her an apologetic smile. "You have been an excellent servant."

"I have been?" She looked to Tanner and back to the doctor. "What does that mean? Where am I going?"

"It means that I've agreed to sell your remaining four and a half years to the man Mister Tanner represents. Pack your things. You will be leaving with him immediately."

"Where am I going?" She turned to Tanner. "Who is buying me?"

"My employer has given me strict orders that neither his name nor his location are to be revealed, not even to Doctor Fayssoux." He gave a huff. "I know this is abrupt, but like Doctor Fayssoux just told you, we will be leaving immediately. Pack your things and meet me outside where a carriage is waiting for us."

Becky turned, ran through the hallway, and down the stairs to her room. While she quickly folded her things and set them into her single suitcase, Mary stepped into the small room.

"What's the matter, Becky? I heard you run past the nursery, crying."

"I've been sold!"

"Sold? Why?"

"I don't know. Doctor Fayssoux would not tell me."

"What have you done now?"

"I don't know." She stopped packing and wiped the tears from her face. "None of it makes sense."

"What happened?"

"There was a man at the market who kept watching and following me. I thought I lost him, but when I returned with the groceries, he was waiting for me in the alley."

"Then he already knew where you lived."

"That's right!" Rebecca looked back toward the hallway. "I figured he was nothing more than a secret admirer but to show up here, and to know that I would enter through the alley gate…"

"Did he say anything to you?"

"He called me by name, and then he reached into his coat for something. That's when I rammed him with the cart and hit him the one of the fish."

"What happened then?"

"I ran through the yard to the kitchen. Margie brought out two cleavers and she went back out with me to pick up the food. When we got to the alley, the man was gone. But then Mister Conway summoned me to the master's study. The man was there with Doctor Fayssoux."

"Oh, Rebecca." Mary began to sob. "What am I going to do without you?"

Rebecca put her arms around the younger woman and gave her a comforting squeeze. "You'll be alright, Mary. These people love you, and Lady Fayssoux is pregnant again."

"Will you write to me?"

"Yes—if I am allowed."

CHAPTER EIGHT:
The Sloop Liberty

Rebecca returned to the doctor's study with Miss Taylor and her bag of belongings. Susan stopped in the hallway and turned to Rebecca. "Wait here, Becky, and try not to cry."

"But this is as bad as when they forced me to send Joshua away to slavery."

"I know it must feel like that but—"

"What if it was happening to you? What if you and Grady were engaged and then some stranger came and took you away?"

"You're right." Susan put an arm around Rebecca. "We're both believers, Becky. God knows what is happening to you. You have to trust him that there is good somewhere in this."

"I know I should be more trusting, but this goes against everything that I was hoping for."

Jeremy Tanner stepped to the door. "Your housekeeper is correct, Rebecca. Your new life will be difficult at first, but you will quickly see that my employer is a fair and just man, and that—"

"Look at this!" She held up her hand. "Joshua gave me this ring the morning that we were to be married. Then I was forced to send him away."

"Yes?"

"He promised that he would come back for me, and I won't be here when he comes." She looked to the doctor. "When Joshua comes looking for me, please promise me that you'll tell him where I have been taken."

"I'm sorry, Becky. All I can tell your young man is that your remaining years have been purchased and that you were taken away today." The doctor stood and walked to the young woman. "As much as I would like to tell you who he is and where you are going, I truly do not know."

She pointed at Jeremy. "But he knows."

The doctor put a hand on Rebecca's arm. "Your four and a half remaining years are being purchased for double what I paid for you. Part of the agreement is that your destination and the name of the man be kept a secret, even from me." He took a large breath. "I wouldn't have considered doing this, but there are greater things going on here than either you or I are privy to."

"What things?"

"I'm sorry, Becky. I am constrained as much as you."

Jeremy took Rebecca's bag. "Be quick with your goodbyes. I will be waiting at the carriage."

Susan followed her down the stairs to the courtyard. "Where is he taking you?"

"They won't tell me, Susan."

"What's going on, Becky?" Margie stepped from the kitchen. "Are you being arrested?"

"It's worse, Margie."

"How could anything be worse than that?"

"She's been sold." Susan gave Rebecca a hug.

"Sold?" Margaret looked to the carriage. "Why in God's name would the doctor sell you?"

"It's complicated, and I wish I had more time to tell you." She looked to the carriage. "He owns me now, and I must go."

"You'll write to us, won't you?"

"Yes, if I am allowed."

"If you're allowed?"

"Mister Tanner made it clear that nobody is to know the name of my new sponsor or where I am being taken."

"This is terrible."

"Rebecca!"

"Coming!" With a last kiss, Rebecca turned and ran through the gate where she was helped into the carriage. Jeremy turned to Susan and Margaret. "Do not follow us."

The two stood in the middle of Tradd Street and watched until the carriage was out of sight. When they returned to the courtyard, Samuel Pain was standing in the alleyway just outside the back gate.

"Susan! Margie!" He pushed through the gate and met them next to the kitchen. "I have great news. Becky and I had a talk this morning while she was on her way to the market, and we have come to an important agreement."

"What agreement?" Susan looked at Margie and back to Samuel. "She told me that—"

"I'm making good money now, and it won't be long until I can redeem Becky—the remaining years on her contract." He looked up at the doctor's window. "I just need to talk to Doctor Fayssoux to find out how much that would cost me."

"Oh, Lord!"

"What?"

"Becky's gone." She turned and pointed back at the front gate. "A man just did what you are proposing."

"What?"

"A man just paid the doctor for her remaining years of service."

"She's free?" He looked from one to the other. "Joshua came back and redeemed her?"

"No." Susan put a comforting hand out toward him. "It was a King's solicitor. He was hired by somebody to buy her remaining years."

"Why?" He looked toward Tradd Street. "What did he want in return?"

"He wanted Becky."

"He took her away?"

"Yes—not five minutes ago in his carriage."

"Where did he take her?"

"The man would not tell us when we asked."

"Which way did they go?"

"East—toward the bay." Susan pointed. "But they could have turned and gone another direction."

Without another word, Sam ran to the gate, turned, and ran forward with all his might toward the docks.

☠ ☠ ☠

Jeremy Tanner's carriage stopped where a man was waiting on the dock. He stepped to the carriage as Jeremy climbed down. "Is this her, sir?"

"Rebecca Keyes, this is Billy Wilson, one of my crewmen." While the man carried Rebecca's bag down to the waiting boat, Jeremy assisted her aboard and took his place at the rudder. He gave a nod to the young man.

"Please." She turned to the seaman. "I don't suppose you are allowed to tell me where we're going, either."

Billy gave Tanner a quick glance and began rowing without comment. A hundred yards ahead stood a large and finely appointed sloop that carried no guns. The name on the stern read, *Liberty*. As the boat bumped against the boarding ladder, two seamen reached down and helped Rebecca aboard.

"Captain Morton!" Jeremy held up a hand to the man. "As soon as the boat is aboard and secured, raise your anchor and get *Liberty* underway!"

"As you please, Mister Tanner."

Jeremy led Rebecca to a cabin where there was a bath tub, soap, and fresh clothing. "Wait here until the bath tub is filled, and then clean yourself up." He pointed to several garments on the bed. "Those are your new clothes. In an hour—when you are more presentable—someone will bring you to me."

"I'm not filthy, Mister Tanner. I bathed last evening."

"It's the new clothes. I'm sure you would prefer to be freshly bathed."

"And then you'll tell me what this is about?"

"Yes." Two sailors stepped to the cabin door with buckets of hot water. "Ah! Your bath."

While she was thus occupied, the ship put out to sea. As promised, Rebecca was ushered into the master's cabin where the man stood behind one of two chairs. "Please. Have a seat and we'll talk."

"Three questions before I join you."

He waited behind her chair. "Yes?"

"Who are you? Why have you purchased my remaining bonded years? Where are you taking me?"

"I'm a King's solicitor, and I was paid to acquire you." He paused. "I am taking you to your new master."

"I will not sit." She looked at the food on the table. "Nor will I join you at dinner until you tell me why my new master has done this to me."

"Please." He nodded to the chair. "If you'll sit down, I promise to answer your questions."

"Very well." She sat down.

"The man who hired me sent me to Charles Town to find him a certain woman."

"A certain woman?" She pointed back toward the town. "That means Doctor Fayssoux and he did this together."

"No—they never met, nor do they know about each other."

"Then what does that mean—*a certain woman*?"

"This." He handed Rebecca a framed painting of a woman. "This is—was—his wife, Kathleen. They were married five years and she was killed in a carriage accident."

"Oh, my. She and I could have been twin sisters." She looked up at him. "Is this why you chose me—because I look like her?" She looked at the picture again. "He's trying to replace Kathleen, isn't he?"

"He insisted that I bring him a young woman from the south—from Charles Town if possible.

"Why?"

"Kathleen was born and raised here. He was hoping to find a young woman with the same southern charm."

"Ha! Then the joke is on both of you."

"The joke?"

"I'm the daughter of a lowly English domestic—a man who tends the livestock and the gardens. I was born thirty miles south of Lambeth where I worked the land with my hands. I have no South Caroline blood in me—much less the genteel blood of a so-called Southern Belle." She gave a tilt of her head. "I hope he's already paid you, because when he learns the truth—what you have brought him—you won't get the rest of your money."

"I already knew that about you—where you came from."

"So, it was my looks that made you choose me?"

"Your physical appearance was naturally the first thing that I noticed about you, Rebecca, and then I began to overhear your conversations with the merchants and the advice you gave to the other shoppers."

"Ha!" She pointed back toward Charles Town. "Then—when you were about to offer your proposal in the alley, I attacked you."

"Actually, that was the clincher, as they say."

"You still wanted me after I rammed you and hit you with that grouper?"

"Not only do you have physical beauty, but you are both smart and courageous."

"There had to be something else."

"I'll admit that you were one of several young women I was watching at the public market."

"Tell me about them. Why me and not one of them?"

"It…" He glanced at the painting.

"So, I looked more like Kathleen than any of the others?"

"My employer did not require that you had to look like her, but like I said, your looks were a great factor in my decision."

"Why don't we muck this stall and dump the horse manure where it belongs?" Tanner gave a nod. "If I promise to lie for you—to play the perfect Southern Belle—what will you do for me?"

"I…"

"No!" She held up a hand to silence him. "*I'll* tell you what you'll do."

"What?"

"You'll be my nearest and dearest friend, the friend who goes out of his way to help me whenever, wherever, and however I need his help."

It took him a long moment before he nodded. "Yes. I will do whatever you ask as long as it does not break the law or hurt someone."

"When we reach our destination—wherever that might be—you will send a letter to Doctor Fayssoux and tell him where I have been taken, and the name of the man who owns me. You will tell the doctor that when Joshua comes to Charles Town looking for me, to give him the letter."

"Yes." He nodded. "I will do that."

"Good!" She struck a provocative pose and affected a southern accent. "I will be what your master hopes I will be. I will be that Southern Belle that he has paid for, oozing all the charm and respectability he paid for."

"What will you do if he asks for your hand in marriage?"

"I'll face that problem when and if it happens."

"I would imagine that you have more questions to ask me, Rebecca."

"Oh, yes."

"Can we eat now?" He gave the steward a nod.

"Wait!" She held up a hand to the steward. "First, tell me when Doctor Fayssoux learned about this—that you came to Charles Town to buy my remaining years of servitude?"

"It was four days ago."

"Then he knew and didn't tell me."

"When I first noticed you, I followed you home. Then I followed the doctor to his clinic to present my employer's offer."

"Since we are finally being honest with one another, and we are now at sea, tell me who your employer is, and where he lives?"

"I suppose…" He poured them each a glass of light wine as the steward returned with the tray of food. "My employer is Francis Faulkner. He owns and manages a textile company at Acton, Massachusetts. He is in his mid-twenties, and a widower with no children." He spread his arms. "This sloop—the *Liberty*—is one of four ships."

"What happened to his wife?"

"I wasn't told much about her other than it was a carriage accident that took her life."

"That's it?" She sat back and spread her arms. "A rich young widower paid for all this—to send you in this pretty sloop to buy the daughter of a lowly slave of the land?"

"He has had agents in both Savannah and Philadelphia, along with other cities throughout the colonies, looking for a woman who fulfills everything he desires in a wife."

"Which one am I?"

"Pardon?"

"Am I the first woman he's done this to—bought my remaining years so he can test me—or am I just one of many?"

Jeremy gave her a shrug. "Unless one of the others has preceded us, you will be the first."

"What happens to me if I'm not the one he wants to marry? Am I to be sold back to the family at Charles Town?"

"No. You'll remain in Colonel Faulkner's employ and be taught what you need to know to become a rich and powerful woman, provided you are able to apply what you learn."

She pointed to larboard. "We've turned north. Are you allowed to tell me our destination?"

He nodded. "Boston."

CHAPTER NINE:
Colonel Fracis Faulkner

*U*pon the *Liberty's* arrival at Boston, Rebecca was taken by carriage straight to the small town of Acton and her new master's home at 5 Hill Street. Mister Tanner had supplied her with new clothes, and her hair had been done up in lazy curls to match the woman in the painting.

"Please remain here, Rebecca, while I conduct my business with the colonel"

"How will I know when to go into the house?"

"I'll be leaving for Boston in this carriage." Jeremy walked quickly to the front door and knocked. He was met by Francis.

"Welcome, Jeremy." He looked to the carriage. "I see that your quest was a success."

"Yes, and you will be well pleased with the young woman I found."

"Come!" Francis backed away and gestured for Jeremy to join him in the parlor. A moment later, he poured two glasses of whiskey and put his hand on a money box. "There is one matter that must be dispensed with before I can pay your fee."

"Oh?" Jeremy set his glass on the desk. "Is there a problem?"

"While you and the young woman were debarking, a courier was sent to me by horseback from the docks."

"Does it concern me?"

"He carried a letter from Captain Morton that told of a conversation relayed to him by the cook."

"What conversation?"

"The cook heard you promise to send a letter to Doctor Fayssoux telling him my name and location so that when her betrothed comes looking for her, the doctor can tell him." He waited. "Did you promise to do that?"

"Yes—she made me promise."

"She *made* you promise? How so?"

"Your instructions were that I bring you a young woman who was born and raised in or around Charles Town—a Southern Belle. Rebecca Keyes was born to a family of serfs near Lambeth, England. They were driven off the land when it became more economical to raise sheep than vegetables. Rebecca indentured herself to Charles Town with her betrothed, but the young man was sold into slavery."

"Hmm. Where was he taken?"

"Rebecca doesn't know. Somewhere in the Caribbean—most likely Cuba or Hispaniola."

"What did Rebecca promise you in exchange for your promise?"

"She promised that she would play the perfect Southern Belle like you requested." Jeremy took a large breath and let it out slowly. "I won't write the letter. Doctor Fayssoux will never know where Rebecca has been taken."

"If you ever tell him, you will be sued for breach of contract. You will forfeit the money I have paid you plus your entire earthly worth, and you will be disbarred from the legal profession." Francis pushed the money box across the desk but kept his hand in place. "Do we understand each other?"

"Yes, sir." Jeremy took the metal box and stood. "Shall I send her in?"

"Yes—to the parlor. Tell the footman to have her wait there for me."

Jeremy walked to the carriage and helped Rebecca down to the gravel driveway.

"Well?" Rebecca released his hand. "Is Colonel Faulkner ready to receive me?" Jeremy looked at her for a long moment. She could tell something was amiss. "What's wrong?"

"It's…"

"He doesn't want me after all, does he?"

"He is looking forward to meeting you."

"But there's something." She glanced to the house and back. "What has happened?"

"It's a personal issue between the colonel and me." He nodded toward the house. "Go. He wants you to wait for him in the parlor."

She was met in the foyer by a man on his late forties. "Miss Keyes, I presume."

"Yes." She expected a younger man. "Are you him?"

"I'm Spencer—the colonel's butler." He pointed. "Please take a seat in the parlor. Colonel Faulkner will be down in a few minutes."

"Thank you." Rebecca looked around the palatial room. The walls were cheery panels beginning at the top of the wainscoting and continuing upward to the picture molding. From there to the ceiling was a cove and then another delicate strip of molding. The ceiling was bone white with blue floral designs at the four corners. A display case was filled with pistols, presentation swords, and letters of commendation—each with an intricate crest and ribbon attached. Four paintings of army officers adorned the walls.

Footsteps came down the carpeted stairs. A man slightly taller than Joshua stepped to the door and stood for a long moment. He stood six feet tall and was of solid stature. His hair was coal black and tied back in a military queue. His features were refined but assertive, resembling a drawing of Patrick Henry that Rebecca had seen in Charles Town.

"My name is Francis Faulkner." He stepped forward, took her hand, and kissed it. "I am pleased to meet you, Rebecca."

"Before you go any further, Mister Faulkner, you must hear me out."

"Yes?"

"I know I have an obligation to you, but by all rights, you owe me an explanation for what has happened to me these past several weeks."

"I know how bewildering this must be for you, but hopefully I can explain why I used this method for bringing you here. I instructed Mister Tanner not to tell you anything but…"

"He told me your name, the business you own, and that you live here in Acton."

Francis led her to a chair. "Please have a seat, Rebecca."

"Thank you." She gave him a studied look.

"Like I said a moment ago, my name is Francis Faulkner. I am a Colonel in His Majesty's Army. I will turn twenty-six in a few months."

"That makes you eight years older than me."

"But I want you to know about me—who I am and what I hope to—"

"Why do I need to know *anything* about you?" She gave him a tilt of her head. "You own me for the next four and a half years, unless you plan to do this to me again—sell me off when you tire of me."

"Please indulge me, Rebecca." He waited. Finally satisfied that she would listen, he continued. "I inherited a vast sum of money and real estate holdings in England when my brother and four cousins were killed in the French and Indian wars. I wanted to grow the inheritance, so I invested a great sum of my money with Lewis Paul and John Wyatt. They own a cotton mill at Upper Priory, and at my insistence, we now get our cotton from the Ediston and Ryley Company in Savannah."

Rebecca gave no noticeable reaction, so he continued.

"I have commissioned James Hargreaves of Oswaldtwistle, Lancashire, England to build me twelve of his new invention—the Spinning Jenny—so that we Americans can begin producing our own cotton thread. I am also looking into the woolen and worsted suppliers in Scotland, but that will have to wait until my factory is at full production." He pointed north. "I have located a good piece of property next to the Assabet River where I can use the steady flow of water to power the factory." He gave her a smile. "My factory will be only fifteen miles from Boston Harbor."

"Why me? There must be hundreds of young pretty women here in Boston. Why didn't you choose one of them?"

"None of them were quite right." He gave a nervous laugh. "This sounds terrible of me, doesn't it? I'm speaking as if you are nothing more than a slab of meat on display at the public market."

"That's where your hired man—Jeremy Tanner—found me." She gave him a long look as each of them took measure of the other. "What's next? Do you send me off to your kitchen to prove that I can cook, or is it as Jeremy Tanner told me—that you brought me here to replace your recently departed wife?"

He looked at her for a long moment and then nodded. "Jeremy is correct."

"During our two-week voyage from Charles Town, Jeremy stressed that I must play the part of a Southern Belle, but I can't be a part of his deception." She leaned forward in her chair and spoke in a cold and determined voice. "My name is Rebecca Keyes. I indentured myself at the Lambeth docks along with my betrothed, Joshua Smoot, with the understanding that we would be married at sea and then serve our seven years together at Charles Town. The captain—Michael Drake—lied to us. As we suspected, his son Edwin had designs on me. Edwin staged a fight with Joshua. The outcome was that Joshua's future was placed in my hands. My choice was to watch him hanged that very day, or have him transferred to a slave ship headed to one of the Caribbean islands." She shook her head. "I have no idea where they took him."

"That is truly unfortunate, and depending on how that still affects you, you may or may not qualify—"

"You're right. I may not qualify to be your wife."

He sat back. "You don't like—"

"This!" She spread her arms. "The way you did this, ruins everything!" He sat silent. "Joshua believes that I am somewhere in Charles Town, and since neither the doctor nor anybody in his household knows where I am, how will Joshua know how to find me?"

"I understand your dilemma, Rebecca."

"You own me for another four and a half years, and you have the intent that if I measure up to your standards, that I become your wife. In slavery, only the master has the power of consent. Marriage is a covenant and must be by the mutual consent of both the man and the woman."

"Go on."

"As long as there is a chance that Joshua will return, I cannot marry you."

"And what if you receive word that he is dead?"

"If that happens—if I discover that he is indeed dead—then you may court me."

He smiled. "Not only are you beautiful, but I perceive that you are both intelligent and wise." He stepped to the desk, pulled a piece of parchment from a wooden tray, dipped a quill, and wrote for several minutes. When he finished, he held out the quill. "This will require both our signatures."

She turned the document around, scanned the words quickly, and looked up at him.

"You're willing to pay the price of his redemption from slavery?"

He nodded. "Yes, if we can find him."

Rebecca dipped the quill into the ink bottle and held it over the parchment. She hesitated. "He's been a slave for as long as I have been indentured. If I'm going to find him alive; I must leave for the Caribbean immediately.'"

"Where would your search begin?"

"I…" She shook her head. "Cuba, Jamaica, and Hispaniola. Places where they have slaves."

"There is slavery even in this country. He could have been sold to Florida or one of several other southern colonies."

Rebecca just looked at him.

"There's a better way to find him."

"Oh?"

"Do you know the names of the captain and the slave ship that took him?"

"It was the *Crow* under the command of Michael Drake."

"There's a Lloyd's of London office in Boston. If they insured that ship, they would have the records of its voyages and ports of call."

A week later, a dispatch arrived from the insurance company. Francis opened it and read it to Rebecca. "Lloyd's of London lists four ports of call for the slaver *Crow*. The first is Baracoa, then Matanzas, Puerto Escondido, and finally Havana."

"Does the report give any details about who the slaves were or where they were sold?"

"It lists the human cargo as eighty Africans and seven Englishmen convicted of crimes."

"Is he named? Is Joshua named as one of them?"

"A moment." He scanned down the paper and looked up at her. "Joshua's name is not here."

"But I saw them take Joshua aboard the *Crow*." She bit her lip. "If they killed him, would he be listed as lost at sea?"

"Baracoa: One Englishman named John Manley with one Negro named Simbatu." He skipped down. Matanzas: Eighteen male Negroes and sixteen female Negroes."

"John Manley!"

"What? Is that name familiar?"

"Joshua was raised in the stables by John Manley, and that's the name he wrote on the indenture papers at Lambeth."

"Then if he's still alive, he's a slave at one of the sugar cane plantations near Baracoa."

"How soon can we leave?"

It…" Francis thought quickly. "It will take me a week to get everything in order at my mill and to provision *Liberty* for the cruise." He gave her an assuring look. "We'll leave at the earliest possible moment."

"Thank you, Francis." She looked to the hallway. "Until then, I'll—"

She was interrupted by the butler. A young man with a flintlock rifle stood back several feet. "Sir. One of your men is here with an important message."

"Thank you, Spencer. Show him in."

"Good afternoon, Colonel." He looked at Rebecca. "Please excuse my intrusion, but this is important."

"It's alright, Mister Chandler." He gave Rebecca a quick glance. "What word do you bring me?"

"I've recruited fourteen more able-bodied men for the militia, and there's word that the British are taking an odd interest at both Lexington and Concord."

"Thank you."

"Do you have any orders for me to pass on to the men, sir?"

"No, not until we learn more about what the British are up to."

The man gave a salute and left.

"You're a Colonel in His Majesty's Army, and you are forming a militia against him? Isn't that treason?"

"There's a revolution coming, Rebecca. The British Sovereign has…" He fell silent. "Your only concern is the search for your betrothed."

CHAPTER TEN:
Search at Baracoa

One week later, Francis and Rebecca set sail for Cuba aboard his sloop, *Liberty*. As they passed Florida, Captain Morton stepped to the gallery and knocked on the doorframe.

Francis looked up from his card game. "What is it, Tom?"

"We've a Spanish ship approaching from the southeast, sir. Do you want me to take evasive action?"

"Hold your course. I'm coming up." He set down his cards and stood. "It's probably nothing, Rebecca. I'll be back as quickly as I can."

"I'd like to go up with you."

"Of course." He took her hand and helped her up the ladder and across to where the captain was studying the Spaniard through his telescope.

"Can you make out their name yet?" Francis shaded his eyes and looked to port.

"Not yet, sir, but the way they seem to be floundering, I will in a moment."

"Please—the spyglass." He took the telescope and scanned the approaching ship. "That's strange."

"It is most strange, isn't it, sir?"

"They're only using one sail and the main gallant is twisted cockeyed on the mast." He looked to the captain. "What do you make of that?"

"It's only a guess, sir, but she looks to be a military ship. That would mean most of her crew are soldiers who know nothing about sailing."

"Ah. That would explain it." Francis raised the telescope for another look. The sailors are trying to teach the soldiers the ropes, and it's not going well."

"Can you make out a name yet, sir?"

"Yes—just coming into view now. She's the *El Pescador*."

"The Fisherman." It was Rebecca.

Francis lowered the telescope and looked at her. "You know Spanish?"

"A little—enough to buy food at the market."

"Do you want to remain topside, or finish our card game?"

"I'd like to use the telescope, if you don't mind."

"Of course." He handed her the instrument.

Rebecca scanned the ship and saw a man looking back at her through his telescope. "Are we friendly with the Spaniards?"

"I believe so, but one can never count on political alliances from one month to the next."

She continued studying while calling out. "Captain Morton, do you know how much longer before we reach Baracoa?"

"If these winds hold, we should arrive by noon tomorrow, Miss Keyes."

By now, *El Pescador* had turned her stern toward *Liberty*. Rebecca lowered the telescope and looked at Francis. "I'm..."

"If Joshua's alive, we'll buy his freedom, and I will perform your marriage ceremony en route back to Charles Town."

"You would do that for us?"

"Of course but if he's dead—"

"Please, don't say that."

"Face it, Rebecca. It will be what it will be."

☠ ☠ ☠

The *Liberty* was met by mostly the women and children of Baracoa. There was one fat man among them, and he met their boat as it skidded onto the sand.

"Welcome to Baracoa!" The man rubbed his bulging stomach as he studied the occupants of the boat in the hope that they had brought him a slave or two. "I am Ricardo El Arriaga." He turned and pointed at the tavern and the other several shops. "I run the waterfront. I buy and sell everything that comes here by ship."

"Oh?" Francis stepped into the ankle-deep water and helped Rebecca to the dry sand. "What does that mean?"

"It means that if you have anything you want to buy or sell in Baracoa, I am your man."

"And what kind of things do you buy and sell?" Francis could see the corner of a bamboo cage that stood behind the last shop and pointed. "And what do you put in that cage?"

"Ah, the cage." Ricardo gave a laugh. "Criminals, animals, slaves, and anything else that needs to be kept from harming the good people of Baracoa."

"Ah-ha." Francis looked back at *Liberty*. "So, if we did happen to have two or three slaves aboard our ship, you would be the man we would sell them to?"

"Yes—there is nobody else who buys and sells slaves." Ricardo licked his lips in anticipation. "Men slaves are worth more than women slaves, and they must be strong and healthy."

"And when you auction them off, where do the men go?"

"They all go to the sugar plantations."

Rebecca put a hand on Francis' arm. "Do you keep a record of the slaves you buy and sell?"

"Of course." He gave a suspicious look at the two. "Are you looking for a certain slave to buy?"

"Yes." Francis pulled the paper from his vest pocket. "His name is John Manley. He was brought here on the slaver *Crow* over two years ago. We are prepared to pay you double what he brought on the auction block."

Ricardo took a step back and looked from Francis to Rebecca. He opened his mouth but did not speak.

"Well?" Francis held up a leather bag of coins and gave them a shake.

"Come with me." The fat man turned and walked to the shop next to the cage. Once inside, Ricardo pulled a journal from the bookcase and set it on his desk. "Ah. John Manley." He put a finger on the notation and looked up at the two. "I remember the day he and the Negro Simbatu arrived."

"Enough of this!" Rebecca slapped a hand on the journal. "Who did you sell him to? Where is he?"

"According to my record, it was the plantation of Don Santana." He looked up. "If I weren't so busy, I would take you there."

"How much?" Francis reached into the leather bag and drew out three silver coins.

"That would be—"

"No!" Before Ricardo could take the three coins, Rebecca pulled her knife and stabbed it into the pages of the journal next to the coins. "Take us to him, now!"

The fat man picked up the coins and gave a nod. "My wagon is out back. It will take a few minutes for me to hitch up the horses." He put the coins in his pocket and set a bottle of rum and two glasses before the couple. "Enough time for a little rum while you wait?"

"No, thank you." Rebecca twisted her knife free. "We're not letting you out of our sight until we find John."

An hour later, the three rode up to the hacienda of Don Santana where they were met by two servants.

"If you two will climb down, I will take my horse to the water trough."

While the two waited for Ricardo to return, an elderly man stepped through an arbor from the garden. "I am Don Santana. May I help you?"

"We are here to enquire about one of your slaves."

"Oh?" Just then, Ricardo walked back around the corner of the hacienda. "Gordo! How long has it been, my friend?"

"Just over a month ago when the *Leopard* brought me those three new Africans." He gave a laugh. "They were the right price, but Lady Santana didn't want them."

"Right!" He looked at the two. "And who are these two fine looking guests?"

"We are here to buy one of your slaves—a young white man named John Manley."

"I don't know the names of my slaves." He looked to Ricardo. "Do you remember this, John Manley?"

"Ricardo's journal recorded his sale to you two and a half years ago. Where is he?"

"I don't keep track of the slaves."

"Who does?"

"My factor—Alazar."

"Take us to him."

"I don't like your tone, ma'am." He looked to Francis and back to Rebecca. "You come to my home without invitation, and now you are demanding that I tell you about one of my slaves."

"Stop." Francis pulled Rebecca back. "Let me explain." He took a breath. "John Manley and Rebecca Keyes indentured themselves in England over two years ago and were to be taken to Charles Town after the captain married them at sea. But there was trouble and John was sent here as a slave." He turned to Rebecca. "She—we are here to right a terrible wrong, and are willing to pay you double John's worth."

"Ah! I see it now. This is a matter of the heart." The Don turned to Ricardo. "You can take your cart and return to the bay. I will take these two to Alazar's house and stay with them until they find John Manley."

"As you say, Don Santana."

Don Santana turned and called. "Pedro!"

The servant ran to the three. "Sir?"

"Prepare my carriage."

"Yes, sir." The servant left.

"I must apologize for what has happened to you, Miss Keyes. Had I known this the day I bought John, I would have set him free and paid his passage back to Charles Town."

"It's not your fault, sir. And neither is it the fault of Ricardo or the captain of the *Crow* who brought him to Baracoa."

"This is all true, and I am hoping that John is still on my plantation somewhere."

Pedro returned. "Sir, your carriage is ready."

Ten minutes later, they arrived at Alazar's modest home.

"Don Santana!" He stood from his lunch and wiped his mouth. "What brings you to my humble home?"

"One of your slaves—John Manley—where is he?"

"He died of the cholera over two years ago with the others." He went to his book case and took down a journal. It took a moment. "Here." He pointed at the entry. "Their bodies were burned and their bones were buried with the rest of the diseased debris in a mass grave."

"Dead?" Rebecca walked to the man. "What happened? I want to know everything."

"It was that first season, right after the cane was cut and gathered for processing. Cholera swept through the camp and killed most of our workers—slaves and the indentured servants alike."

"You're certain John was among those who died?"

"Very certain, ma'am." Alazar gave a nod. "He and that Ethiopian friend who was sold to Don Santana were trouble-makers. I remember the two very well."

She looked at Francis. "This…"

"We've done all we can, Rebecca." He looked to Don Santana. "Will you take us back to our ship."

"Of course."

While Francis and Rebecca walked ahead to the carriage, Alazar touched Don Santana's arm. "Sir, a word before you take them back to the harbor."

"Does it have anything to do with John Manley?"

"He and those other seven did not die of cholera as I wrote in my journal."

"What? You lied?"

"They were taken to a beach while the dead were burned along with their huts. My guard had no idea how they escaped, but in the morning, they were gone."

"Why did you do that?" He pointed to the carriage. "I must tell those two that John may be alive somewhere."

"No—you must not do that, sir."

"Why not?"

"Your reputation, sir?"

"What about my reputation."

"It is common knowledge that slaves never run away from the Don Santana's sugar plantation."

"But they have run away—several every year. That is why we are always buying new ones to replace them."

"True, sir, but the other plantation owners believe otherwise and envy you." Don Santana just looked at him. "You must maintain that reputation at all cost."

"I hate this, but you are right, Alazar."

Two hours later, Liberty weighed anchor and sailed away toward Boston.

CHAPTER ELEVEN:
The Near Miss

*E*l Pescador arrived at Charles Town just after lunch and sailed toward a line of ships at anchor. Not knowing how he was supposed to conduct himself, Joshua decided to drop his anchor near the other ships and see whether it caused any trouble. He did not have to wait long.

"Ahoy, *El Pescador*!" A man in a uniform called from a row boat. "You can't anchor here!"

"Why not?" Joshua could not see anything wrong with the location. "Those other ships have done the same."

"You're flying a Spanish flag." He pointed. "Your kind anchor out there."

Joshua looked east. Two other ships—one flying an Italian flag and the other flying a French flag—were anchored several hundred yards back toward the sea. "Is Britain at war with those nations?"

"Not at war, but the politics in Charles Town is such right now that your kind are out of favor."

"What if I paid you some money? Would that put us in favor?"

It took the man a moment. "Ten pounds and you can stay where you are for two days and two nights, but then you must move out with the others."

"Very well!" While the harbor master approached, *El Pescador*'s boat was lowered to the water.

Joshua held out the money. "There's one other thing, and then you can have this money."

"What would that be?"

"When a ship brings indentured servants into Charles Town, is there a place or a person who determines where they are sent to fulfill their seven years?"

"Aye." The man held out his hand for the money but did not answer until Joshua released it. "When you get to the docks, there is an office with a red sign over the door and the words Sidney Baker, King's Solicitor. That is where you will find the information you need."

A half hour later, Joshua and Simbatu sat before an elderly man with an open journal. He looked up at them. "Rebecca Keyes, Mary Stewart, and a new-born named Joshua Stewart went to the home of Doctor Peter Fayssoux at 126 Tradd Street."

"Thank you, sir."

Joshua and Simbatu were met at the door by the butler. "May I help you?"

"I'm John Manley. I was indentured with Rebecca Keyes two and a half years ago, but we were separated."

"Oh my."

"I know it's been a long time, but I promised Rebecca that I would return for her."

"Please." The butler ushered the two into the parlor. "Take a seat while I get Doctor Fayssoux."

"Something's wrong, Joshua." Simbatu gave a shake of his head. "That man would be getting Rebecca before he would be getting the doctor."

"Yes, I agree." The two could hear the butler and the doctor in a lively conversation, and then the rapid footsteps down the stairs. "Something is terribly wrong."

"So, you're John Manley—Rebecca's betrothed?"

"Please. May I see her?"

"It's been more than two years since she came to us. What took you so long getting here?"

"Michael Drake—the captain of the *Maiden*—allowed his son Edwin to force me into a fight—"

"Yes. Becky has told us the story several times, but she didn't know what happened to you after you were sent across to that slaver."

"I was sold into slavery at Baracoa. I spent five months before eight of us escaped during a cholera plague. We fled to Hispaniola and joined a clan of buccaneers. We did that for two years, and then the King of Spain sent his soldiers to find and kill us. We fled to Tortuga but they followed. In desperation, we took their ship and escaped to the open sea. We sailed straight here." He looked to the butler and back to the doctor. "Is that enough? May I see Rebecca now?"

"I'm so sorry, Joshua, but Rebecca is not here."

"Not here?" Joshua instinctively put his hand on his pistol. "Where is she?"

"Several weeks ago, a solicitor came and bought her remaining four and a half years of servitude."

"You sold her?"

"The man paid triple what I paid to sponsor her."

"Where did he take her?"

"We were not told."

"Who was he? Do you know his name?"

"Jeremy Tanner, and he was under the strict orders of his employer that he not tell me or anyone else where Rebecca was being taken."

"So, she's alive." He looked to Simbatu and back to the doctor. "How did they leave? By carriage or by ship?"

"They left in a carriage, and we did not follow them."

"What about me?" Joshua hesitated—not sure that he should have asked. "Did you pay for my passage also?"

"No." He shook his head. "A sponsor only pays when he receives the indentured servant at his home."

"Then I owe you nothing—neither the seven years nor the cost of my passage to America."

"From what you and Rebecca have told me, you have more than paid for your freedom."

Joshua stood and backed toward the door. "I have taken more of your time than I should."

"What will you do now?"

"I don't know. There are people who need killing, but I have no idea where they are."

"Taking revenge will not decrease the pain you have suffered, John."

"No, but I can hope that it will make the guilty hurt as much as I have."

When Joshua and Simbatu reached *El Pescador*, one of the crew was looking through the spyglass at one of the ships in the anchor line. "Captain Smoot!"

"What do you see, Grady?"

"You told us that the ship that took you and that girl you loved from England was the *Maiden*." He pointed. "Look—the third ship from the end."

"It's them!" Joshua lowered the spyglass and continued looking at the ship.

"What are we going to do, Captain?"

"I'm going to go kill Edwin Drake and his father."

That night just before midnight, Joshua, Simbatu, Alan, and Grady pulled across the bay and slipped aboard the *Maiden*. Once on deck, Joshua lowered his lamp and whispered to the three. "Stay here in case his crew hears me and comes up." He pulled his knife and looked about the empty deck. "This will only take me a few minutes."

Joshua knew the ship well, and the beds the two occupied. With his knife held between his teeth to free his hands, he pushed his way silently into the main cabin, looked around, and whispered. "Good. You're both here."

He set the lamp on the table, stepped to Michael's bed, and put the tip of his knife under Michael's chin. The man awoke with a start.

"Please!" The man screamed. "Mercy! For God's sake, have mercy on me!"

"Michael Drake, tonight you and your son Edwin shall die at the hand of the man you sold into chains and slavery!"

CHAPTER TWELVE:

Savannah Reunion

Clancy MacDonnell walked together with Alana, his new bride, through the gathering mist and across the green grass of the Scotland Highlands—he in his tartan plaid, brass buckles, and kilt—she in her brilliant white muslin dress. The sun was just rising, and with it, the fragrance of the dew-covered flowers and the trill of the melodious meadowlarks. They stopped for a moment to kiss, followed by a prayer of thanksgiving to their Lord and Creator for the blessings given to them. But then the birds stopped singing and burst into the morning sky in an explosion of panic. As the two froze and watched in amazement, the dappled birds grew dark and became ravens—ten at first, and then quickly multiplied into hundreds and then thousands. And as the two continued to watch in horror, the ravens became a dark and ominous cloud with flashes of lightning and explosions of thunder that echoed through and over the mountains. Clancy turned to his bride, but she was gone. Where her hand had been was his battle ax, and the other hand held his leather shield. An English soldier clad in red with two white bands that crossed his chest raised his broad sword and called the Scotsman a profane name. As the outraged soldier attacked Clancy, he could hear others screaming and begging for mercy. What started as a dream of love was now a nightmare of ripping flesh and the breaking of bones. Blood splashed in his face as a sword was thrust at his chest. He swung his ax and the thing was dashed aside for a moment but came back with a renewed fury. Clancy was now on the ground, his tartan wrapped about his fighting arm. The sword blows kept coming and then the deadly blade was at his throat.

"Please!" The Scotsman screamed for his life. "Mercy! For God's sake, have mercy on me!"

Joshua pulled back his knife at the thick Scottish brogue and brought the lantern up so he could see the man's face. "Who are you?"

"I'm…" The frightened man pulled at the sheet that was twisted about his arms. "I'm Clancy MacDonnell!"

"What are you doing in Captain Drake's bed?"

"I don't…" The confused Scotsman caught his breath. "Wait! Where's Alana? Where did they..?"

"I'll ask you again. Why are you in Michael Drake's bed, and who is that in Edwin's bed?"

"That's my son Tommy!" He struggled to get up to make sure his son was alright. "Captain Drake paid us to watch over the *Maiden* while he's away!"

"Away? Where did he go?"

"I don't know. Some sort of family business."

"Did he say where?"

"I don't know that either—just that he paid my son and me to live aboard his ship for two months."

"But you saw him—you spoke with him, right?"

"No, it was his son, Edwin"

"Edwin!" Joshua put his knife back in its sheath. "Are any of his crew staying aboard with you and your son?"

"No—just the lad and me." Clancy gave an apologetic huff. "I know I'm not being very helpful, sir but—"

"It's not your fault."

"You were here to…" Clancy touched his throat. It was wet with blood. He looked at his hand. "You came aboard to kill them, didn't you?"

"Did you see where Edwin went after he paid you?"

"We were on the dock. He got in a large, closed carriage and left."

"Was his father with him?"

"I don't know. He might have been in the carriage. I don't know."

Did you see which way they went?"

"No." Clancy shook his head. "I have no idea whether they went north or south, or whether they're still someplace here in Charles Town."

"North of south?"

"After they left, several of his crew were talking about how they would travel. I heard them mention Boston, Fredericksburg, Richmond, and Savannah." Clancy shook his head. "I think one or two were staying in Charles Town, but I have no idea who they are or how you could find them."

"Savannah?"

"There were three, and they spoke of crewing on one of the coasters to work their way down there."

"If Edwin returns in the next few days, send word to my ship." He pointed seaward. "The *El Pescador*."

"I will."

For the next two days, Joshua searched the docks and the various taverns for a sign of Michael and Edwin Drake, or for anybody who knew where they might have gone. Either nobody knew, or they simply refused to tell.

Finally giving up the search, Joshua returned to *El Pescador*. "Simbatu, call the men to the deck." Ten minutes later, the clan of buccaneers stood about their captain. "Make ready. We're sailing to Savannah on the tide."

Two days later, Joshua sailed *El Pescador* up the Savannah River to Flint's Creek and dropped anchor in deep water next to the mud-bound and rotting *Walrus*. The old ship's stern was intact, but the scrolled board that displayed its name had fallen and lay in the mud. Joshua and Simbatu were rowed ashore and set onto a makeshift dock next to the hulk.

"Look there, Joshua." Simbatu pointed to two men walking inside a Roman-style water wheel that was pushing water from the Savannah River into the creek. "Strange, that two white men are doing what black men usually do."

"My guess is that they are either working off an indentured debt, or they have been ordered to hard labor for a crime short of the gallows."

Joshua walked across the field and watched them for a moment. "That looks like hard work. How much are you being paid to do it?"

"Nothing, because it's this or the gallows for both of us."

"Really?" Joshua gave Simbatu a raise of his brows. "Who are you, and why do you fear the gallows?"

"My name is Isaac Attucks, and this is my younger brother, Aaron." The two stopped walking in the wheel and stepped up on the levy. Isaac pointed up at a building on the cliff. "We work for Constable Damon Hobson."

"What is he holding over you?"

"He caught us poaching John Flint's deer when we were young, and since then, he has accused us of many more crimes."

"And how many of these crimes did you commit?"

"None, but he claims that he has enough evidence to convict us, and we have no way to clear our names."

"Nobody would come to your aid?"

"We're orphans. At first, we were moved from one home to another—from one kind family to the next. As we got older and could work, we were able to feed ourselves, and we slept where people didn't care."

"None of them would help you?"

Isaac shook his head. "The problem is that the people who helped us are just as afraid of Hobson as we are."

Joshua turned and looked up at the building. "I see."

"Hey!" Aaron pointed at El Pescador. "You came in on that Spanish ship, didn't you?"

"Yes. I'm Joshua Smoot, her captain."

"It's you?" Isaac gave his younger brother a push and turned back to Joshua. "You're John Flint's son?"

"Yes, and I'm not proud of it."

"This is his creek—Flint's Creek!"

"Really?" Joshua looked to the rice fields. "Can you tell me how I can find John Flint."

"Oh, you can't find him, sir."

"Why not?"

"Because he died some time ago—six or eight years ago—maybe more."

"Do you know where he is buried?"

"No." Aaron shook his head. "Rumor has it that he was buried in secret by his shipmate, Long John Silver."

"Is his grave somewhere here in Savannah?"

"Yes, but the same rumor has it that neither of the two churches would have him because it would desecrate their sacred ground."

"Then how does a person find this Long John Silver?"

"That's as big a mystery as where John Flint is buried." Aaron gave Joshua a questioning look. "If you're figuring on visiting his grave to pray over him, I'd say you should not waste your time."

"It isn't to pray for him, Aaron. It's to dig him up and throw his carcass out onto the mud flats so I can watch the crabs pick his bones clean."

"You hate him that much?"

"Yes, and if he was still alive, I would kill him and let the carrion creatures have a fresh meal."

Aaron turned and pointed at Joshua's ship. "That's a Spanish caravel, isn't it?"

"It's Spanish, but I don't know enough about ships to call it that."

"Did you bring anything to sell to the merchants?"

"Yes—why?"

"Well, this is the wrong place for that."

"And where, pray tell, is the right place?"

"There." Aaron pointed west. "The merchants and townsfolk buy and sell at the cotton docks a half mile up river. When you're ready to do that—sell your cargo--you'll want to move your ship up there."

"Thank you for the information." He gave Simbatu a nod. "Let's go back and get the ship moved."

An hour later, *El Pescador* lowered its gang plank and welcomed the town of Savannah aboard.

"Simbatu, can you oversee this for me?"

"Aye, Captain." The Ethiopian looked to Alan. "Between Alan and me, we'll make the crew rich." He called after Joshua as he jumped down to the dock. "If we need you, where will you be?"

"There's a small home on the west side of town. I was born there, and I want to see if the place is still standing."

"Should we expect you back tonight?"

"Yes, unless something prevents me."

Joshua walked out to West River Street and set off at a quick pace. After three blocks, a young woman called and stepped into his path. He tried to step around her, but she countered his moves. "I know what you are. If I wanted female companionship, I know where to buy it."

"Oh, no, sir. I am not a prostitute but I—"

"Then you're a common beggar!" He reached into his coat pocket and held out several coins. "Tell me where the midwife Emily Smoot used to live and I will give you this."

"Don't you recognize me, Joshua?"

"How do you know my name?"

It's me. Sarah...Sarah Smoot."

"Sarah?" It took Joshua several moments. "Oh!" He took her into his arms and kissed her cheeks. "My sister, Sarah!"

"Where have you been all these years, Joshua?"

"In exile." He pointed east toward his ship and turned back to her. "It's a long story."

She took his hand and pulled him up the road past several other small homes.

As they got close, he pulled loose and looked up and down the familiar road. "We played here every day." He pointed at a green home with a thatched roof. "I set that roof afire when I was six."

"Yes, and you got a royal spanking for doing so, and then mother made you repair everything that burned."

"What happened to Scupper, that cat that begged food from everybody? Is he still around?"

"No. An eagle got him."

"Too bad." He stepped to the picket fence that circled Sarah's home and put his hands on two of the pickets. "This is where you taught me to walk, and later to count my numbers."

"I was there, but you were so determined to walk that you taught yourself." She gave his arm a pull. "Come inside." She walked up the steps and pushed the door open. "I kept everything the way it was that day John Flint killed mother and took you away."

"Really?" He followed through the small doorway into the main room and came to a sudden stop. "There!" He pointed at a throw rug. "That's where he killed her!" He fell to his knees and took hold of the edge. It would not move. He looked up at Sarah. "It's stuck."

"When they came for her, I set that rug over the place where she died so I wouldn't have to look at her blood." She gave him a pained look. "I'm sorry, Joshua. I was going to wash it away, but after it dried, I couldn't bear to touch it."

"Where does that kind of evil come from?"

She put a hand on her forearm. "It's this flesh we occupy while we're alive."

"What?" He looked up at her. "We aren't all as evil as John Flint."

"When our flesh is cold, it demands warmth. When it is hungry, it kills to eat. When it is tired, it sleeps." She held up her hand and ticked off the fingers. "Almost everything we do is to satisfy this flesh. Evil men will take what they want to satisfy longings with no concern for the people they take it from, even if it means killing them."

"I see that." He stood and walked to the table. "What John Flint did was more than to satisfy his hungry flesh."

"God gave us all the animal desires we share, but He also told us to control ourselves."

"You aren't saying that John Flint is not to blame for killing our mother, are you?"

"No." She shook her head. "I've tried to figure it out, Joshua, but there is no logical reason for doing what he did, especially in front of us."

"Maybe that's exactly why he killed her—to show me that he was serious about what he intended for me." He spotted the seaman's chest under the window. "Ah! Our toy box!"

"Yes, and I saved everything."

"My horse and my windmill?"

"Yes, but what I have to tell you is much more important than some old toys." She stepped to the bookcase and put a hand on the row of journals. "Can you stay the night?"

"I need to get back to my ship."

"But you have a crew that can protect your ship."

"It's something I have to do, and it doesn't concern you."

"But it does, Joshua. Everything that has happened to you concerns me." She gave his hand a gentle squeeze. "Where did John Flint take you?"

"To England—to a large estate to the south of London. He paid a man to raise me up as a gentleman."

"A gentleman?" She looked at his clothes. "But word from the docks is that you're a pirate just like John Flint."

"When I refused to take the name of Thomas Flint, Lord Lyddell sent me to the stables and ordered that I be treated as a slave. When I was sixteen or seventeen, I got into some trouble and ran away. I met and fell in love with a girl named Rebecca Keyes. When she and her family were put off the land, I followed her to Lambeth where we ran into more trouble."

"What kind of trouble?"

"I broke a pickpocket's fingers when he tried to steal my things, and then to escape a flogging, Rebecca and I indentured ourselves to a family in Charles Town." He doubled up his fists. "But the captain and his son turned on us."

"What did they do?"

"The captain promised that he would marry us once at sea so that we would not be separated when we reached Charles Town."

"Then you and Rebecca are married?"

"No!"

"Why not? What happened?"

"He helped his son falsely accuse me of attempted murder so that he could have Rebecca for himself."

"Oh, my."

"The devil of a man forced Rebecca to choose my destiny. She was given the choice that I be hung from a yardarm or be sent away as a slave."

"Oh, Lord!"

"What?"

"So, this captain and his son were doing to you what John Flint did to your father and mother."

"My father and mother? Are you saying that I am not John Flint's bastard?"

"That's what I am trying to tell you."

"But—"

"You found Rebecca, right?" She pointed. "She's on your ship right now waiting for you, isn't she?"

"No."

"No?" She gave him a questioning look. "But they took her to Charles Town."

"Yes. She was working at a doctor's home, but after two and a half years, somebody came and purchased her remaining years of servitude."

"Where did they take her?"

"Nobody knows." He gave Sarah a dark stare. "While asking around at Charles Town, we happened upon the *Maiden*. We went aboard to kill the captain and his son, but they were not there."

"Why would he leave his ship at Charles Town?"

"The man who was paid to watch his ship told me that the captain was badly injured and came to Savannah to recover from his wound."

"And you're here to kill him."

"Yes."

"Please, Joshua. You need to hear what my mother told me about your mother."

"Then tell me?"

"Our mother was one of Savannah's three midwives." She pointed at the row of journals lining the bookshelves. "Those journals record all the births she assisted—each marked for the years it contains, but she had another journal—a personal journal she kept in a secret place with her money."

"Yes—I remember you and her talking about this stuff a lot, but it really didn't matter that much to me." He gave a laugh. "I was too busy stepping on bugs and teasing the stray cats and dogs."

"You were just a little boy, and that's what little boys do."

"But now I'm a man, so tell me about her personal journal."

"It was my mother's collection of secrets, hopes, and dreams. It was also a detailed record of everything that happened to your mother—Elaine MacBride—from when she was a little girl to her honeymoon trip to America with her new husband. It told where she lived in Scotland, about her mother, their unwanted pregnancy, the rushed wedding and trip to America that her mother arranged, and finally your birth."

"Did it describe John Flint's attack on their ship?"

"Yes—that terrible day when John Flint attacked the Fortune and took her for himself while setting David adrift with the crew that were not killed." She reached across and took Joshua's hand. "Mother showed me your mother's last will and testament that left everything to you."

"Where is it—this personal journal and my mother's will?"

"She hid it. When I asked her why I couldn't know where it was, she said that John Flint might try to force me to tell him." Sarah shook her head. "I have searched everywhere, and for the life of me, I can't find it."

"Then it might as well not exist, which takes me back to Damon Hobson's story that I am John Flint's bastard."

"There's something else."

"What?"

"This." Sarah held out her hand to him. "This was your father's wedding gift to your mother."

He took the thing and held it up to the light. "It's a crest of some sort." He looked up. "Is this important?"

"It's your family crest—your family in Scotland."

"If he gave it to her, then it's mine now, right?"

"Yes but..."

"Fine!" He stuck it through his ascot. "But what?"

"Don't you remember the story our mother—my mother—always told over and over about you and your real mother?"

"Vaguely, but the words of a dead woman and a little boy mean nothing in court of law."

"You aren't suggesting that she might have made it all up, are you?"

"She lied to John Flint, didn't she?"

"Only to protect you."

"And then Flint lied to me—that he wouldn't hurt my mother anymore." He pointed across at the row of numbered journals. "Then he held that page in her face—the one that he tore from that dated journal—and then he shot her."

"Your mother—Elaine MacBride—died shortly after she gave birth to you from blood loss. Right after she wrote out the will, she begged my mother to do two things." She turned and pointed at the dated journals. "The first was to record that you were a stillborn girl. The second promise was that my mother would record that you were her baby and that she would raise you as my little brother."

"What if Hobson has your mother's journal and my mother's will?" He shook his head. "He would have burned both of them the moment that he read them."

"I know." She gave a defeated sigh. "Mother told me that Hobson came here every week to check on Elaine. That's how he knew that only your mother was pregnant and my mother was lying to protect you."

"Without that journal and the will, there is no proof who my real father is." Joshua took a large breath and let it out slowly. "Why did he take me when he could have taken any one of his other bastard sons to England?"

"I found out the reason." She gave a shake of her head. "You were the only boy."

"My mother must have reached out for help to her family in Scotland."

"Mother told me that she wrote several letters to her mother—your grandmother—but she never wrote back and nobody ever came."

"That doesn't make sense."

"She was pregnant with you before they were married, and her mother was somebody very important in Scotland."

"That must be it. The family must have decided that they couldn't face such a scandal."

"That's what your mother thought, so she gave up all hope."

Joshua got up and stepped to the toy chest. "Enough of this." He raised the lid and picked up his wheeled horse and his windmill. He carried the two toys to the table and sat back down. "I remember playing with these."

"Aye." Sarah turned and gave him a warm smile. "When you were just a toddler, we would sit across from each other and push that horse back and forth."

"This was also a favorite." He picked up the windmill and gave the sails a spin, causing a bell to tinkle. "Who made these?"

"Our mother got them from a Dutch immigrant when you were little—when you were about four years old." She spooned some stew into a bowl and brought it to him. "Here. This is our mother's recipe. You'll remember it."

Joshua turned the windmill over. A name was scratched into the base. "Willem Kesteren." He looked at Sarah. "Do you know if he still makes toys?"

"Oh!" She pointed west with the ladle. "I do know who that is."

"He's still here in Savannah?"

"Yes, but now he mainly builds houses, barns, and warehouses in and around Savannah."

"Do you know where he lives?"

"Why?" She looked at the toy. "Is your windmill broken?"

"No."

"Do you want something built?"

"I…" He turned the fan on the windmill again and smiled at the tinkling bell.

"What is it, Joshua?"

"Give me a moment." He continued to turn the sails around as he thought. Finally, after several more rotations, he looked up at her. "There are two young men working at a water wheel at Flint's Creek."

"I know them well. Isaac and Aaron Attucks. They work for that man—Constable Damon Hobson—the man who brought John Flint here the day he killed my mother and took you away."

"What do you know about them and the locks built along the creek?"

"Hobson claims to hold several King's warrants over their heads and uses the fear of the gallows to force them to work for him." She waited, but he didn't answer. "Everybody in Savannah knows what Hobson has done to those two."

"Since John Flint is dead and I'm his son, the creek is mine by inheritance."

"And?"

"I need for you to tell me how to find Willem Kesteren." He turned the sails on the toy windmill again. "The Dutchman who built this."

"He has a small office up near the cotton warehouses at the docks, but he's usually at his lumber yard just south of the last wards."

Sarah brought her bowl of stew to the table and sat down. After a short prayer, she looked up at him. "Have you tasted it yet?"

"Yes, and you're right. I remember it well." He took another spoonful and chewed. After several more bites, he set down his spoon. "Those two men working at Flint's Creek told me a short while ago that my father—that John Flint is dead—and that he was buried by one of his shipmates, a man named Long John Silver."

"We've all heard the same story."

"Then…" Joshua thought for a moment. "If you've heard the same stories, then you must know where he's buried."

"It's no secret that he died here in Savannah, but nobody knows where they laid his body." She gave him a questioning look. "Why do you want to know?"

"Why?" He turned and pointed at the throw rug. "He killed our mother right there as we watched!"

"I know that, Joshua, but John Flint is dead and burning in hell. Why do you need to know where his body is buried?"

"Somebody must know."

She shook her head. "There are only two graveyards in Savannah, and neither of the ministers would allow John Flint's body to desecrate their hallowed ground where the Saints rest."

"Then how do I find this Long John Silver?"

"I've never met the man, and except for a story about a treasure on Spyglass Island, I know nothing about him."

"Okay—another question."

"Yes?"

"What do you know about Michael and Edwin Drake—the two men I came to kill?"

Sarah covered her mouth. "Edwin Drake? What dealings have you with him?"

"He's Captain Drake's son—the one I was telling you about who made me a slave and took Rebecca away from me." He sensed she knew more. "Do you know him?"

She nodded slowly as her eyes filled with tears. "He forced himself on me nearly a year ago."

"He raped you?" She nodded. "Then you have just as much reason to kill him as I do."

"I know but—"

"What is it? Is he blackmailing you?"

"No. It's just that—"

"Then why wouldn't you want him punished?"

"I'm a Christian. The Scriptures forbid me taking vengeance on him."

"Another Christian!" He sat back. "I would be the one killing him, not you."

She shook her head. "I don't think God would see it that way."

He grabbed her wrist in his calloused hand and squeezed. "Tell me!"

She winced in pain and tried to pull away. "You're hurting me, Joshua!"

"His location, Sarah." He eased his grip but held her fast. "What I do to Edwin Drake when I find him is on me, not you."

"If you kill Edwin for what he did to me—"

"He'll die for what he did to Rebecca and me." He released her wrist. "Your God will punish his soul after I kill him—if he has one—for what he did to you."

"But…"

"Edwin must pay the price for his behavior, whether he did it to a Christian like you or a heathen like me." Joshua took several more bites of his stew.

"When did you last see Edwin Drake?" He waited for her to answer, but there was only silence. "Sarah?"

"When I reported the rape to the constable—to Damon Hobson—Edwin and his father conveniently left Savannah before they could be arrested."

"A year ago? You haven't seen or heard of them for a year?"

"No."

"I'm going back to my ship." He stood and walked to the door. "If you hear anything about the Drakes or Long John Silver, or you find Emily's journal and my mother's will, send me word." With that, Joshua pulled back the door and was gone.

CHAPTER THIRTEEN:
Agreements and Promises

"*H*ello on *El Pescador*!" The man was short and overweight but dressed well. He cupped his hands about his mouth and called again. "Hello! Is there anybody aboard!"

One of the buccaneers looked over the rail to the makeshift dock. "Who are you, and what do you want?"

"I'm Basil Lamar! I'm here to represent the Savannah merchants to your captain!"

"The sale of our cargo is finished. If you missed it, that's your fault!"

"I—we have an offer for Captain Smoot!"

Just then, Joshua stepped down from the carriage behind the man and handed the driver several coins. "I'm Captain Smoot. What kind of offer, Mister Lamar?"

"Is there a place where we can sit down together?"

"Come aboard." Joshua helped the man up the narrow gangway and across to the companionway. Once in the master's cabin, Joshua opened a box of cigars and uncorked a bottle of Madera. "I assume you imbibe."

"Yes, thank you."

"So, how can we serve each other?"

"It's a delicate matter." The little man took a large breath. "Savannah has always…"

"Get to it, sir."

"John Flint used to bring us his swag for pence on the pound. We provided him and his crew a safe haven while he helped the town prosper." He took a sip of his wine and put the cigar into his vest pocket. "Would you consider doing what your father did for us?"

"My father…" Joshua fell silent. "My father was a pirate. You know that, of course."

"Yes?"

"And you want to know whether I am a pirate also?"

"We…" Lamar took another sip of his wine. "We're not trying to trap you, Captain Smoot—accusing you or piracy. We simply want to know whether you would be willing…"

"I know what my father did, and I can see the obvious benefits for both Savannah and my crew if I choose to continue that relationship with you."

"Then, you're willing to consider it?"

"Of course, I am."

"Then, can I tell my associates that we have an agreement?"

"Not until I do some research."

"Research?" Lamar gave a tilt of his head. "It's a straight forward arrangement. You bring us ships that you have taken at sea, and we buy both the ships and their cargoes."

"There are other questions that concern me—things that I do not as yet have the answers to."

"I know everything about Savannah. Ask me the questions here and now so we can remove any obstacles you believe may yet stand between us."

"Be patient, Mister Lamar."

"The men I represent will expect me to give them an answer when I return to them. What shall I tell them?"

"You can tell them to be patient, and that I will speak with them after I do my research."

"May I ask what kind of research?"

"No." Joshua stood. "Where will I find you when I have an answer?"

"Here." Basil handed Joshua a piece of paper. "If I'm out, you can leave a message accountant."

"Good. I'll be in touch."

Once the man was gone, Joshua and Simbatu set out for the Kesteren Building Company. It was located a quarter mile south of the last ward and was a bustle of activity. The office stood over the warehouse with a clear view of the entire construction yard.

Joshua gave a light knock and pushed through the door. "Excuse us. We're looking for Willem Kesteren." He held up the windmill. "The man who made this."

"Yes." The elderly man at the desk looked up from his journal. "I'm Willem Kesteren, and you're Captain Joshua Smoot."

"Is that a good thing or a bad thing?"

"I'm a businessman, not unlike yourself. I get paid for making things—big things." He gave a smile. "You're a pirate. If you are anything like your father, you get paid to capture and sell enemy ships and their cargoes to the merchants of Savannah."

"You know more about me than I know about you."

"Then have a seat and let us talk." He took the windmill from Joshua and gave the sails a spin. "If it's about your toy, there's nothing wrong with it."

"My sister—Sarah Smoot—told me that you immigrated from Holland, and that when you were there, you built several windmills."

"Your sister is correct."

"Could you build a windmill for me?"

"Hmm." He turned the toy around in his hand. "I designed and built four windmills in Holland and operated one of the four. After I came to Georgia, I apprenticed for a short time at the company that built the river docks for James Oglethorpe. Then, with the financial help of several friends, I started my own building company." He spun the sails on the toy. "How much do you know about the windmills of Holland?"

"I know that some of them ground grain into flour, but most of them moved water."

Willem gave a smile. "There's a saying in Europe. *Holland is as flat as a pancake.* The country is actually a huge delta, formed by the sediment of several rivers that dump into the sea. In Holland, a farm is called a polder. If a person wanted to claim a portion of the flooded delta, he would first wall it off, and then build one or more windmills to pump the land dry. After a month or so, the man had his own polder."

"But doesn't water always seep back where it came from—from a high place to a lower place?"

"Yes, and that is why the windmills in Holland have to run every day." He turned the toy windmill over and looked at his signature. "Why would you want me to build you a windmill?"

"Are you familiar with the rice plantations on the flatlands east of the town?"

"Of course, I am. I helped build that system of locks that hold or release the water from the river."

"I am John Flint's son. That makes me his sole heir and owner of his Flint's Creek." Joshua hesitated—waiting for an objection that didn't come. "I want to control the movement of water to and from the rice plantations."

"Ah-ha!" Willem got up and stepped to an alcove. He made a quick search. "Here!" He brought a sealed tube to his desk, removed one of the end pieces, and dumped out a large, rolled parchment. "These are the plans for the last windmill I built in Holland." He pointed at a tube that went down into the water. "That's an Archimedes Screw—the heart of the machine."

"Who is Archimedes?"

"Nearly three-hundred years before the birth of our Lord, Archimedes was born in Syracuse, Sicily. He was schooled in the classical Greek subjects but went on to become one of the world's greatest mathematicians, physicists, engineers, astronomers, and inventors. During a trip to Egypt, Archimedes observed a device that lifted water from a low place to a high place. It was a tube with a helical internal body that—when turned—carried the water upward. Archimedes made detailed drawings and took the idea back to Greece where the water pump was employed for the same purpose."

"Then it was the Egyptians—not Archimedes—who invented the pump?"

"Actually, there is strong evidence that these pumps were used long before in the hanging gardens of Babylon and driven by slaves walking in treadmills."

"Like those two—Isaac and Aaron Attucks."

"Yes, much like that contraption."

"My father brought his swag to his anchorage at the creek entrance and sold it to the merchants for pence on the pound, thereby avoiding the British taxes." Joshua studied the plans for a long moment. "I was visited by Basil Lamar today. He wants me to take up where John Flint left off, and he is willing to negotiate with me to accomplish that. I want to someday be able to dock my ship at the creek instead of at the cotton docks."

"Damon Hobson claimed ownership and control of the irrigation system when your father died. Am I correct that you are going to take that away from Hobson?"

"Yes, and before I present my demand to the merchants, I need to know whether you could build me a windmill to pump the water in and out of the rice fields."

Willem took a clean sheet of parchment from a stack and started drawing. After ten minutes, he stopped and turned the drawing around to the two. "Before you agree to anything, consider what I've drawn here."

"This is…"

"To do what you want, you'll need to dredge the river so that your ship can pull up to a dock. With a dock like this, you will also want several warehouses to store the various commodities you will handle."

"Commodities?"

"The windmill will do more than run an Archimedes screw."

"Oh?"

"Give me a moment." The man drew for another five minutes and then looked up. "Since your main object is to pump water into and out of the canal for irrigation, the windmill must be built over the canal in a deep section near the river."

"Okay?"

"Here's the important part." Willem sat back. "Rice has a certain growing season—April to October if I am correct—leaving much of the year with no need for your windmill to turn."

"I see that." Joshua watched as Willem drew another diagram. "What are you drawing now?"

"With a simple shifting of certain gears in the drive train of the mill, the wind—which blows all year long—can just as easily drive a sawmill and a grist mill." He put his hand on a map of the Savannah River. "That is why you will need the docks and warehouses."

"You can do that?"

"Yes, and the additional revenue will pay for the modifications in the first year of operation."

"What would that cost me?"

"Many thousands of dollars, but it will take me a while to work out the details."

Joshua picked up the drawing. "Can I take this with me to show to Basil Lamar and his associates?"

"Yes."

"Thank you, sir. We will be in touch."

On the way to his meeting with the merchants, Joshua and Simbatu stopped at Damon Hobson's office. "Good afternoon." Joshua stepped in out of the hot sun. "Are you Constable Damon Hobson, and the factor of Flint's Creek?"

"Yes." The little man nodded and gave a proud smile. "I'm also in charge of the workers and everything they do in the fields."

"An important position, I'm sure."

"There are fifteen of them—all answering to me." He looked Joshua up and down and glanced across at Simbatu. "Are you and your man looking for work?"

"No." Joshua thought quickly. "I am on a quest."

"What are you looking for?"

"I'm looking for several people, one of which carries a reward."

"A reward you say?" Damon licked his lips. "I know everybody in Savannah, and for a price, I will tell you where they are."

"I was told by one of those I've already found that two of my acquaintances—Isaac and Aaron Attucks—work for you. Have I been told correctly?"

"Ah! The two poachers!"

"Pardon?"

"I caught the two lads red-handed a dozen years ago, killing one of John Flint's deer, and I've convinced them that I know about other laws that they've broken." He gave a smile. "The two are certain that I have enough to send them to the gallows." He turned and pointed up at an arrow hanging from the rafters by strings. It was encrusted with dried blood. "See that? That's the very arrow they used to kill John Flint's deer." He gave another laugh. "It's easy to hold a fool in servitude."

"So, they aren't very smart?"

"Actually…" Damon leaned close as if he might be overheard. "The only thing I have on those two gullible fools is that bloody arrow, and since John Flint is dead, that poaching charge means nothing anymore."

"Are they here?"

"Yes." The little man stepped out into the sun, walked to the cliff, pointed to the north end of the rice fields, and called back to Joshua. "That's them at the water wheel!"

"Fine." Joshua turned and started toward the horse cart where Simbatu waited but stopped and turned back to the little man. "Did you work for John Flint?"

"Yes. I was the broker between him and the merchants who bought the goods he brought to Savannah."

"Do you happen to know how I can find Michael Drake and his son Edwin."

"Five dollars." Damon gave a nod and rubbed his thumb against his fingers. "I know of them, but it will take me a while to find them. Come back tomorrow with my money."

"I'll pay you after you tell me." Ten minutes later, Joshua and Simbatu descended the hill and reigned the horse to a stop near the water wheel. Simbatu pointed. "There they are—resting."

"Isaac! Aaron!"

The two jumped to their feet and turned. "You're back!"

"I just had an interesting talk with your boss—Damon Hobson. He calls you the two gullible poachers."

"That was many years ago and we haven't killed any of John Flint's deer since. What has he accused us of doing now?"

"Actually, he confessed that except for the arrow, he has nothing on either of you."

"What?"

"He's been lying to you all these years that he has enough crimes against you to send you to the gallows."

"That bastard!"

"I have a proposition for you." Joshua gave the brothers a smile. "How would you like to stop working for Hobson and start working for me?"

"Uh…" Isaac looked to Aaron and back to Joshua. "On your ship? Are you asking us if we want to be buccaneers?"

"No. What I'm offering is for you to stay here in Savannah and operate my windmill."

"There are no windmills in Savannah." Aaron looked at the water wheel. "There are several dozen gristmills, but they are all up river from Savannah and driven by water wheels."

"Look at this." Joshua unrolled the drawing. "The wind will pump the water, and when it isn't doing that, it will run a saw mill and a grist mill."

"Can that be done?"

"Yes." He pointed. "And there will be warehouses on the docks that I will have built."

"When will this happen?"

"I am meeting with Basil Lamar and several of the other merchants this afternoon to establish an agreement like John Flint used to have with them." He held up the parchment. "This windmill, the docks, the warehouses, and you two running it for me. That will be part of our agreement."

"Uh…" Aaron looked around again at the water wheel and the rice fields. "Damon Hobson won't go away willingly." He raised his shoulders as if he was being scolded. "You'd have to kill him."

"Better men have died for less."

"You'd do that? You would kill him for us?"

"If I kill him, it will be for my sake, not for your sake."

CHAPTER FOURTEEN:
Justice for Damon Hobson

That afternoon, Joshua Smoot and Simbatu arrived at the home of Basil Lamar just as the sun was setting. The mood of the six merchants was hopeful expectation while the pirate captain's mood was dogged determination.

"Welcome to my home, Captain Smoot." Basil gave Simbatu a quick glance. "Your servant can remain with your carriage, and if your horse needs anything, my stables are around back."

"His name is Simbatu, and he is a free man."

"But…" Basil turned and looked at the others. "He's a Negro."

"He's a man—as much a man as you and me."

"Of course, he's a man but—"

Joshua put his hand on his pistol. "Simbatu is my First Officer and my closest friend."

"Then…?"

"Simbatu either joins us as an equal—a free human being like me and your little group—or this meeting stops here at your doorstep." Joshua waited for a little too long. "Very well." He turned and started toward the carriage.

"Wait, Captain Smoot!"

Joshua stopped but didn't turn. "I'm listening."

"I apologize for my error. Of course, you can include Simbatu in this meeting."

"And?" Joshua turned back to the embarrassed men. "When he speaks, will you consider his ideas as you would consider mine?"

"Yes, and he is welcome to the cigars and refreshments."

"Then let's do this."

A few minutes later, the eight men took their places at the dining table. Basil began without prompting. "Your father—John Flint—knew how to fool the British so that he could sail his prizes up the river to our docks. As best as I know, he used diversions, and he also put aboard specially trained prize crews who passed as British."

"Go on."

"May I speak?" It was a Mister Mayhew. "With the death of your father, we all but gave up importing the British goods. The Crown levied such high taxes on us to pay for the Indian wars that nobody in Savannah could pay the prices we had to demand."

One of the others—a Mister Lawrence—held up a hand. "Thomas is right, but it gets worse. We send England the raw materials that they change into finished products. Lumber, furs, dried fish, whale oil, iron, gunpowder, rice, tobacco, indigo, and cotton. The only finished product we send to them is rum."

"What do they send you—what are the products you need the most?"

"They send us the things we are not allowed to make for ourselves. Textiles, arms and ammunition, medications, and most of the luxuries that make life in Savannah tolerable. We can feed ourselves, but we are very limited by the King's importations and tax laws."

Joshua gave a nod. "Gentlemen, I will agree to the same arrangement John Flint had with you. When you know a certain ship is due to arrive from England, tell me and I will intercept it far at sea, take the goods you indicate, and then send it here in disguise. I will then sell the goods to you at a fair price, without the British taxes and tariffs."

"Wonderful! We will sign an agreement to that effect."

"There is more that I need." He unrolled Kesteren's drawing and set his toy windmill in the center. "These are the plans for a wind-driven water pumping station that would be built at the entrance to Flint's Creek. It is based on the Dutch windmills that employ an Archimedes Screw that will do what the man-driven water wheel is doing now."

One of the men took the plans and turned them around.

"This is a complicated machine."

"I have already spoken with the Dutchman who knows how to acquire the necessary machinery and build the windmill. My trusted friends, Isaac and Aaron Attucks have agreed to help with the construction of the windmill, and to run the entire operation for me."

"We are agreeable with that."

"I will also be building docks and warehouses at my creek so that ships can bring timber and grain to be milled."

The merchants traded looks and all nodded their agreement.

"As you know, my name is Basil Lamar. I am the fourth generation of Thomas Lamar. He immigrated to America nearly a hundred years ago. In honor of my great grandfather—"

"Please. Let's stay on the topic at hand."

"It's a personal concern, Captain."

"What is it?"

"By force and intimidation, John Flint named the creek after himself."

"Yes—Flint's Creek."

"Savannah should not be associated with that person or his reputation anymore."

"Get to your point, Mister Lamar."

"We will agree to your conditions, including your docks and warehouses but we…" Basil gave the others a quick look for their approval. "I ask that—in honor of my great grandfather—you agree that we give the waterway an official name."

"Let me guess. For tribute to your family, you want to name it Lamar's Creek."

"You would own and operate your mills, the docks, and the irrigation system." Basil gave a knowing nod. "After all, the name isn't as important as the ownership."

It took Joshua only a moment. "Yes—you can have your name change"

"When will this happen?"

"As soon as I have accumulated enough to pay for the construction."

"Then…?" Basil looked around at the others. They each gave a nod. "Good! We have our agreement!"

"There is one other matter."

"Yes?"

"I would like to find my father's resting place."

"It's only a rumor, but word is that one of his shipmates—a Long John Silver—buried him someplace here in Savannah."

"Where will I find this Long John Silver?"

"He was born and raised at Kings Town, Jamaica." Basil shook his head. "If I was looking for the old pirate, I would begin my search there."

When Joshua and Simbatu returned to *El Pescador*, there was a message from Damon Hobson. Joshua read the note and looked at Simbatu. "Hobson knows where Michael Drake is hiding."

Early the next morning, Joshua and Simbatu knocked on Damon's door.

"Yes?" The little man opened the door. "Ah! Did you bring the five dollars?"

"Yes. Do you know where Michael Drake is living?"

"It's on my desk." Hobson turned and shuffled through several papers. "Ah! Here it is!"

Joshua stepped to the desk and took the paper. "You're sure of this?"

"If he isn't there, come back and I'll give you your money back."

"Agreed." He set the coins on the desk.

"You said that you were looking for someone else." The little man took the coins. "Who might that be?"

"Elaine MacBride, and there is a reward for her whereabouts."

"What reward?"

"This." Joshua patted his money bag. "A hundred dollars."

"This is your lucky day, good sir, and mine also." Damon opened the bottom drawer of his desk, pulled out a small strong box, and set it on the desktop. "I have the proof right here."

"Oh?" Joshua watched while the little man unlocked the box. "What proof would that be?"

"She was brought to Savannah twenty years ago." He set the stack of letters in front of Joshua. They were tied in a bundle with a blue ribbon. "These are all or her letters to her mother in Edinburgh."

"How did you get these?"

"I'm the Constable. I have access to the postal traffic that goes in and out of Savannah."

"Then you knew Elaine MacBride?"

"I didn't just know her. I was her keeper."

"Oh?"

"David and Elaine MacBride were on their way here from Edinburgh on their honeymoon when John Flint took their ship as a prize. David was set adrift with the men who survived the attack, and he brought Elaine here to Savannah to be his concubine." Damon gave a proud smile. "Captain Flint paid me to be her custodian, and to bring her to him when he wanted her."

"Where did you keep her?"

"At first at my home, but later on when I discovered she was with child, I took her to a midwife named Emily Smoot."

"She didn't try to escape?"

"I made up some charges with false evidence against her to keep her hostage."

"So, what happened to her after she gave birth to John Flint's child?"

"Elaine died shortly after giving birth to the boy."

"He would be a grown man by now. Do you know where he is?

"Captain Flint took him to England when he was eight, and that's the last that I heard of him."

"So…" Joshua picked up the bundle of letters. "That's all recorded is in these letters to her mother?"

"I assume so, but as you can see by the unbroken seals, they have never been opened."

"Very well." Joshua set the bundle of letters on the desk "Do you like riddles, Mister Hobson?"

"As much as any man, as long as they are not too complex."

"It's a guessing game. I tell a story of something that happened right here in Savannah, and you tell me who did it."

The little man gave a grin and leaned back in his chair. "What's your riddle?"

"There was once a man who grabbed a little boy by the hair, pulled him close, and said these words. 'Look at me, Thomas Flint! I am Damon Hobson—a man to be feared as much as your father! When you started growing in your mother's belly, Flint was done with her. I kept your mother my prisoner, and when she wrote to her family for help, I took those letters. You are John Flint's bastard, and I earned thirty Spanish silver dollars by delivering you to him. Look hard and remember me well Thomas Flint, because I did this to you!'"

"It's you!" The little man reached into an open drawer, grabbed a small pistol, and raised it. "You're Joshua Smoot! You're John Flint's bastard!"

"Aye, and I'm here to take revenge." While Hobson's thumb pulled back the hammer, Joshua grabbed the weapon and forced it under Hobson's chin. "While you burn in hell, you'll have eternity to remember what you did to me." The pistol discharged, blowing away most of Damon Hobson's face.

"Joshua!" Simbatu ran through the door and looked at the dead man. "What happened?"

"He shot himself."

"We must leave before someone comes."

"Wait." Joshua took a blank sheet of parchment from the drawer, opened Damon's journal, and copied the dead man's writing style. When he signed the document, he stood. "There."

"What does it say?"

Joshua held it up and read the three sentences. "Savannah: You all know the evil I have done to so many of you. I can no longer live with this guilt. I am ending my life today, and I am gifting all my earthly belongings to the orphans, Isaac and Aaron Attucks. Damon Hobson."

"Will they believe it?"

"The way he was hated, of course, they will."

"What about Michael and Edwin Drake?"

Joshua picked up the bundle of letters, the money, and touched his vest pocket. "I have the address right here."

CHAPTER FIFTEEN:
The Death of Michael Drake

Joshua and Simbatu knocked at the door and waited. After a minute, Joshua knocked again. "I paid his price, so Hobson would have had no reason to send us to the wrong home." He looked at the paper and up at the address numbers above the door.

"Listen, Joshua." Simbatu cupped a hand to his ear. "There's talking inside. Somebody is here."

A woman in her forties pulled the door open. "Are you from the apothecary with the medicine I ordered?"

"Is it for Michael Drake?"

"I didn't give a name but..." She backed away and started to close the door. "Who are you?"

"I'm..." Joshua reconsidered. "I'm somebody who booked passage on his ship several years ago, and I am here to repay a long-overdue debt."

"I'm Clara—Michael's sister." She allowed the door to open a few more inches. "He is very sick in bed with an infection that threatens his life."

"An infection?"

"He was injured at sea a month ago. The surgeon wanted to amputate the leg at his knee, but Michael sent him away." She turned and looked down the hallway. "He's sleeping right now, and I don't want to disturb him."

"I will most certainly disturb him!" Joshua pushed past her, marched down the hallway, and into the room. The stench of rotting flesh forced them to cover their faces.

"It's you!" The old captain pulled the blanket up to his chin as if it would protect him. "They said you were here, and that you were looking for me."

"Where is Edwin?"

"You're going to kill him, aren't you?"

Joshua drew his sword and put the tip at the old man's throat. "Where is he?"

"Please!" Clara ran past the two to and put her hand on the sword. "Please have mercy on my brother. He's a dying man."

Joshua pushed her hand away and put the sword back at Michael's throat. "Choose, Captain Drake. Tell me where he is or you die now."

"Joshua!" Simbatu pointed at several diagrams and charts on the sideboard. He held up a letter. "Look at this!"

"What is it?"

"A letter from Edwin, along with a map of Jamaica, and the plans for a house."

Joshua stepped across the small room and spread the papers. "Bahia de Manteca."

There was a distinctive click—the familiar sound of a flintlock being cocked. As Joshua and Simbatu turned, Michael raised a pistol from under his bedding, pointed it at Joshua's heart, and pulled the trigger. In that short moment it took for the flint to strike the iron plate and produce the spark that would ignite the gun powder in the flash pan, Simbatu jumped between the two men. The pistol fired and Simbatu staggered back against his captain.

"Simbatu!" Joshua dropped to the floor and gathered his friend in his arms. "Why did you do that?"

"Because…" Blood ran from his mouth onto Joshua's arm. "Because I am ready for heaven and you are not."

"What are you talking about? That ball was meant for me."

"No, it wasn't, Joshua. Our Lord has more for you to do, and it was my time."

Joshua stripped away Simbatu's shirt to assess the damage. The ball had entered the man's chest near his heart. "I'll take you to a doctor! You don't need to die at this demon's hand!"

"No! God is trying to tell you something, Joshua."

"By taking you from me?"

"Think about our conversations—the ones we had in that cage at Baracoa and nearly every night since."

"I don't know what you're trying to tell me, Simbatu."

"And I don't have enough breaths left in me to take you by the hand, Joshua."

"Wait. I remember." It took Joshua a moment. "I understand. Jesus gave his life for all mankind, like you just did for me."

"Yes, and I believe…" The Ethiopian coughed up more blood. "I believe that God will give you back Rebecca Keyes someday." Simbatu gave another cough. "I wanted to see my Africa again, but I am going to a better place." His voice became weak as he gasped his final words. "I will be there waiting for you, my brother." With a sigh, the African closed his eyes and was gone.

Joshua stood, and with a shout, plunged it upward through Michael Drakes throat and into his brain.

It was a heart-broken Joshua Smoot that carried Simbatu's lifeless body out to the carriage. When he reached *El Pescador*, several of his men ran down the plank to meet him.

"What happened, Captain?"

"Michael Drake is dead."

"Good!" Alan stepped to the Black man's body and gave it a shake. "What happened to Simbatu?"

"Captain Drake had a pistol under the covers. Simbatu saw him raise it to shoot me and stepped between us to protect me."

"He took a ball that was meant for you?"

"It was—"

"Loyalty, Captain! It was his loyalty for you, and the rest of us would have done the same!"

"Yes." Joshua looked to his ship and gave a huff. "I know, and I thank you."

"What now, Captain?" The large man looked to the river. "Do we go back to sea?"

"Yes but first to Tortuga."

"Tortuga? Why there?"

"I need more crewmen, and I promised Henry Morgan that if I did not find Rebecca, that I would return for him."

"Then, while you find a resting place for Simbatu, we will make ready to sail."

"Thank you. This should not take me long."

There were two churches in Savannah, and each had a graveyard. Christ Church at 28 Bull Street and the Presbyterian Church at 25 West Oglethorpe Avenue. There were no public cemeteries for those who refused to believe in God, and those heretics lay in graves on private land or along one of the roadways that led in and out of Savannah.

When the two ministers saw that Simbatu was an African, they both refused to allow such a man to desecrate their holy ground. Joshua was tempted to kill both ministers, but after considering the relationship he needed to create with the people of Savannah, he decided to bury Simbatu at sea en route to Tobago—pirate fashion.

Two weeks later, *El Pescador* dropped anchor in front of the Musket's Muzzle Inn. Henry Morgan had watched the sea to east and west every day since Joshua left with the promise to return. When he recognized the ship, he ran down to the water's edge with his meager belongings.

"You came back for me!"

"For you, and as many of the other buccaneers as will join us."

"Yes!" Henry jumped into the air and spun about like a whirling dervish. "I'm a pirate! I told Judas Pottersfield that you'd come back for me!"

"Who's Judas Pottersfield?"

"He came here after you and the others left, Cap'n." Henry pointed down at the beach near the old buildings. "Skidded ashore right there, stayed in the inn, and when a ship came to take him to Kings Town, he gave me his boat."

Joshua looked to the others, grabbed Henry by the upper arm, and led him away. "I need your help, Henry."

"Well, Cap'n, as yer new cabin boy, helpin' ya will be my main job." Henry gave a questioning grunt. "What is it you be needin' help with, Cap'n?"

"You remember me telling you and the others about Michael and Edwin drake—how the two took my betrothed from me and sold me into slavery."

"Aye?"

"Simbatu and I found and killed Michael at his sister's home in Savannah."

"Simbatu?" Henry looked at the ship and the men gathered around the boat. "Where is he?"

"He took the bullet that Michael Drake meant for me."

"He died for you?"

"Yes. He said that he did it because he was ready for heaven and I was not."

"What about Edwin? Did you kill him too?"

"No."

"Why not, Cap'n?"

Joshua held up the papers. "He's building a home at the west end of Jamaica—near Bahia de Manteca."

"So..?" Henry gave a tilt of his head.

"The crew wants to continue to take coasters for the money it will bring them. I need your advice for how to talk them into helping me avenge myself against Edwin Drake."

"Judas Pottersfield taught me about leverage, Cap'n."

"Go on."

"They'd be much more inclined to sail all the way down there to let you seek your revenge if there was something in it for them."

"All they want is gold and silver."

"Let me talk to them, Cap'n. I'll tell them that the Spaniards hid several hundred gold bars at the place."

"I could tell them that lie as well as you, Henry."

"Aye, Cap'n, but comin' from me sorta secret-like an' all, as if you don't know about it…"

"Yes—I see."

"By tomorrow morning, I'll have the crew beggin' you to sail there."

The next morning, Alan came to Joshua alone. "A moment of your time, Captain."

"What is it?"

"The lad—Henry Morgan—was telling us last night that there's a buried treasure at Bahia De Manteca."

"Ha! You believe the lad?" Joshua gave a dismissive laugh. "He also claims to be the great-great-grandson of the real Henry Morgan."

"No, Captain. He has a map."

"So, what are you asking me?"

"We want you to sail there and give us a chance to find that treasure."

"But you were insisting that after we found Henry, that we go back to taking the coasters and selling the swag up at Savannah."

"There's nothing stopping us from taking a ship or two while en route to Jamaica. And the people of that place will probably be glad to buy whatever we have while we search for the treasure."

"Let me think about it."

"Thank you, Joshua."

The next morning as *El Pescador* was readied for getting underway, Joshua called his twenty men to the deck. "Alan came to me last evening with a request that we sail to the west end of Jamaica to hunt for treasure." He paused and searched the men's faces. "Is it just him, or do the rest of you agree?"

"We all agree, Captain!" One of the men called out. "And like he told us— we can still take prizes on our way to that place."

"The famous pirate captain, Edward Trelawney, founded the town. He wouldn't have done so if there wasn't great wealth to be had."

"But the name of the place, Joshua. Bahia de Manteca."

"What of it?"

"It's Spanish for Lard Bay." Several of the others gave a muffled laugh. "They raise and slaughter pigs for their fat."

"And they sell it to the Spaniards."

"Are you sure of this?"

"Aye."

"Very well. I'll do as you wish." He gave Henry a quick glance as he looked up at the flag. "The wind is freshening, so let us raise our sails and be done with this place!"

CHAPTER SIXTEEN:
Bahia De Manteca

En route to Jamaica, *El Pescador* encountered two coasters. One carried a cargo of food, including bags of potatoes, rice, barley, corn, and pumpkins. The second ship had mostly dry goods consisting of bolts of cloth, clothing, pots, pans, table settings, flat ware, various farm tools, and other iron implements. Joshua chose the better of the two ships and transferred all the cargo onto it for the passage to Bahia de Manteca. He released the other ship near Havana along with those men who refused to join *El Pescador*.

The arrival of *El Pescador* and the prize ship was announced with a broadside aimed at Fort Montego that stood on a small bluff a half mile from the bay. When none of the cannons returned fire, the crew gave a triumphant cheer.

There were no ships at the docks—only a dozen small fishing boats. Several of the fishermen stopped stacking their nets, turned, and watched the Spanish ship pull itself to the dock while the second ship dropped anchor in the middle of the bay. Word of the arrivals spread quickly through the town of Saint James. Mothers ushered children from the streets, locked the doors, and then watched the fearful sight from their curtained windows. Several dozen men gathered on the dock as Joshua climbed the shroud and turned.

"I'm Captain Joshua Smoot!" He looked down on the throng and made a quick survey. When nobody stepped forward, he called out. "Where is your mayor?"

One of the fishermen stepped forward, shaded his eyes against the sun and pointed toward a string of shops. "Our mayor is at his shop."

"At his shop?" Joshua turned and looked. "Which one?"

"Abraham is the town jeweler."

"Take me to him." Joshua jumped down to the deck and strode down the gangway. "Be quick about it."

"Your ship is Spanish, but you speak as an Englishman." He looked at the others following Joshua. "If you are not Spaniards, then what are you?"

"We are men on a mission." Joshua pulled his pistol from his sash and pointed it at the man. "If you refuse to take me to your mayor, then—"

"Then you are pirates."

"Yes—we are."

If you're here to hurt us and take our money, then you have come too late, sir."

"Too late?" He made a quick scan of the waterfront and the nearby homes. "What are you saying?"

"The plague—or whatever it was that the rats brought with them—got here before you."

"What is your name?"

"My name is Ferdinand." He gave a bow. "Follow me."

After passing two closed businesses, Ferdinand stopped and pushed through the door into a small workshop. "Abraham, this is Captain Joshua Smoot. He and his crew of pirates are here to sack Saint James."

The elderly Jew turned from his work and looked up at the young pirate. After a long moment, he shook his head and turned back to his work.

"Is he right?" Joshua gave the old man a shove. "Are you the mayor of Saint James?"

"Yes, Captain Smoot." He turned. "I am he."

Joshua pulled open several drawers. There was nothing of value. "If this is a jewelry shop, then where is the gold and silver?"

"Here." Abraham picked up the tray of fish hooks. "These fishing hooks that my son and I make for the fishermen are the only currency we have to buy the food they bring from the sea." He stood, stepped to the door, and looked to *El Pescador*. "You are the first sea captain to dock here since the Spaniards brought us the plague."

"This can't be!" He pushed past the boy and into the storage room. A quick search confirmed his fear. "This can't be. Every town has something of value."

"Something of value?"

"Yes!" Joshua stepped back to the old man. "Where is it?"

"The plague took what little we had."

"And what was it that the plague took?"

"It took over half of our people—husbands, wives, sons, and daughters."

"How many?"

"Before they began to die, we had nearly five-hundred souls in Saint James. At last count, there are only two-hundred and ten of us left." Abraham reached to a box, pulled out a length of iron chain, wrapped it around his wrists, and held his hands out to Joshua. "We have nothing of value except ourselves. If you are slavers, then you can put the rest of us on the slave block."

"How am I to know whether you are lying to me just to hide the town's riches?"

"Come with me, Captain Smoot." Abraham pushed out into the afternoon sun. "Let me show you the thriving town of Saint James."

With several of his men following the two, Abraham led Joshua up a side street and walked toward the sound of a crying woman. "Here. This is a new widow—one of many who has lost her husband." He walked toward two children sitting alone on the curb. The little girl was clutching a doll to her breast and sobbing. "Those who have lost their own children have taken in as many of the orphans as they can." Abraham pointed to the church at the end of the street. "There are three separate funerals going on as we speak—funerals that I cannot attend because the families are blaming me for not doing enough to save their loved ones." He spread his arms. "What can one man do against a disease that has no soul—a killer that cannot be reasoned with?"

"Stop." Joshua grabbed Abraham's elbow and held the man.

"Not yet, Captain Smoot!" He looked to Joshua's crewmen and pointed at several villagers with shovels. "If your men wanted to do something useful, they could volunteer to help those men dig graves for their loved-ones." He gave a cryptic laugh. "Perhaps as they dig, they will find the fabled treasure of Edward Trelawny."

"Alright! I'm convinced." Joshua turned away from the death.

"So, now that you have seen the little that remains of Saint James, what have you decided to do for your crew?"

"They…"

"You came a long way to sack Saint James. Your men will want something to show for their trouble."

"Yes—my men came here to find and take Trelawny's treasure." He pointed toward the bay. "Let's go back to my ship."

"Yes, but before we go, I want your opinion, Captain Smoot." It took Abraham a moment to form the words. "Which is better for my people—slavery or this slow but sure death?"

"Slavery is always better than death, because there is always the hope of someday being set free."

"Well, if that is what you intend for me and the others, then so be it."

"Take me back to the docks, Abraham. I have a foc'sle council to hold."

☠ ☠ ☠

Henry Morgan stood up, looked around at the others, and asked the obvious. "We came to this place to take a spoil, but the way ye're talking Cap'n, that has changed. What is it that ye're asking us to do?"

"We have the cargoes of two merchantmen lying in the hold of that anchored in the bay. The disease that ran through Saint James has left these people decimated and without hope. They need our cargo much more than we do."

"So...?" It was one of the older men. "We came all this way with the promise of Trelawny's treasure, and now you're telling us that we will leave with nothing, not even the prize ship we took?"

"We have the means to replace what we give to these people, and they do not." He pointed up toward heaven. "I am not a man of god, but I have seen things happen that seemed impossible. If god did this—taken what began as a mission to satisfy our animal lusts and changed it into a mission of mercy—then I fear that we run a terrible risk if we counter his will."

"The captain's right!" Henry jumped up, walked forward, and stood next to his captain. "Providence did this! These people need our help, and when the good Lord sees us do it, I think he will reward us with double the booty that we give them!"

It took a while, but one by one, the rest of the crew agreed to the plan. The next morning, everything was taken from the hold and spread along the docks. Henry ran from home to home and told the people what Captain Smoot was doing.

As the last of the food and equipment was taken away, Abraham stepped to Joshua. "I noticed the stick pin on your collar, Captain Smoot. Is it special to you, or just something you took during one of your raids?"

"It was my mother's. She died when I was born."

"Would you allow me to express my thanks for what you have done for my people by making it into a ring for your finger?"

Joshua pulled the pin loose and handed it to the man. "How long would it take?"

Abraham looked to the setting sun. "Noon tomorrow."

"Yes—I'd like that very much."

The next morning as *El Pescador* made ready to sail, Abraham called from the dock. "Is Captain Smoot there?"

"Aye!" It was Henry. "He told me that you'd be coming around noon with something for him! Do you have it?"

"Yes!" The old man held up a small box.

Joshua stepped to the rail. "Abraham! You're early!"

"I worked all night." He held up the box and walked up the gangway to the young pirate. "It's sized for your index finger."

Joshua opened the box and inspected the ring. "Ah!" He slipped it onto his finger. "Perfect! I will cherish this for the rest of my life." After a handshake, Joshua turned to Henry. "Make ready to sail."

☠ ☠ ☠

According to the letter Joshua took from Michael Drake, Edwin was building his home on a rock outcropping next to a river and in a cove approximately twenty miles west of Bahia de Manteca. They dropped anchor just short of the location—a place well hidden from view. After making sure of the directions, Joshua and Henry went ashore in one of the ship's boats armed for revenge.

As the two approached the building site, they could hear the familiar sounds of hammers and saws. Joshua stopped behind a stand of small trees and pointed. "That's him—the white man holding the parchment and talking to those two carpenters." He looked to the bay where a forty-foot Bermuda-rigged ketch was moored to a buoy. "That must be Edwin's ketch."

"What are we waiting for, Cap'n?" Henry pointed. "He's right there—not more than thirty yards away. We can grab him, tie him up, and be back aboard the ship before dark."

"Aye." Joshua pulled his sword. "Now!"

Edwin's back was to the two. One of his workers pointed. "You have visitors, Mister Drake."

"Finally!" He turned, expecting the arrival of the clay pipes that would bring the river water to his home. "Wait! You're not—"

"I'm Joshua Smoot—the man you sent to die at Baracoa!"

"I..." Edwin stumbled backward while he pulled his knife. "How did you find me?"

"I visited your father at his death bed."

"No! My father would never tell you how to find me!"

Joshua pulled the letter from his pocket and held it out to Edwin. "It was the letter and map that you sent to him."

"Then I'm right. Me did not betraying me."

"No, but he was a dead man either way."

"What does that mean—either way?"

"Gangrene was killing him because he refused medical treatment for his leg's rotting flesh."

"Did you kill him?"

"Yes." Joshua raised his sword. "He had a pistol under the covers and shot my best friend."

"So, he died of a sword thrust rather than his rotting flesh." He gave a nod. "It's ironic, but I thank you for ending his life that way." He looked down at the sword. "So, are you going to run me through like you did him?"

"That depends on what you tell me about Rebecca Keyes."

"She rejected my efforts to court her, and all I know is that she and her friend Mary Stewart were sent to the same family in Charles Town." He shook his head. "I do not know who sponsored the two."

"She was at Doctor Fayssoux's home for two and a half years, and then somebody bought her remaining indenture obligation." He pressed the sword against Edwin's chest. "Was that you who bought her?"

"No—it would have been a waste of my money to have a woman who hated me for what I did to you." Edwin spread his arms. "So, what now?" He looked down at the sword. "Is this when I die?"

"My ship is anchored on the other side of this peninsula." Joshua pointed. "I'm taking you—"

"You're not going to kill me for sending you to Baracoa?"

"No. You've been more cooperative than your father." Joshua gave Edwin a push. "Walk."

Ten minutes later, the three emerged from the trees and looked down at the bay.

CHAPTER SEVENTEEN:
Justice for Edwin Drake

*T*he three stood for several moments searching the bay for *El Pescador.*

"Well, well." Edwin gave a laugh. "Your loyal crew has sailed away without you, Captain Smoot." He pushed away the sword and turned. "What now?" When Joshua didn't answer, Edwin gave another laugh. "What happened? What did you do to them that made them abandon you?"

"It's none of your business."

"So, I'm right. You did something so wrong that they decided to maroon you and this lad, rather than wait for you to return with my head."

"Cap'n!" Henry pointed west. "The ketch!"

"Henry's right." Joshua gave Edwin a rough push.

"What now?"

"We are going to row out to your ketch, and then Henry and I will decide what to do with you."

Thirty minutes later, the three climbed aboard the *Seagull*—Edwin's forty-foot ketch. Joshua made a quick survey of the ship and the rigging. "You forced Rebecca to make a terrible choice the very morning we were to be married—that I be sold into slavery or hung from a yardarm."

"So..?" Edwin looked to the rigging. "Since there are no yardarms on this little ship, you can't very well hang me."

"No, and since I don't want to go anywhere near Baracoa or any other town on Cuba where slaves are bought and sold, there's only one thing left."

"So, how are you going to kill me?"

"It depends on how long you can hold your breath."

"You're going to drown me?"

"When the *Crow* reached Baracoa, Captain Sperry tied my foot to the anchor, and threw me overboard." As Joshua spoke, he took a coiled hemp line and tied a constrictor knot around Edwin's ankle. "Like me, you'll have a chance to untie yourself."

"And if I make it back up to the surface, what then?"

"Henry and I will retrieve the anchor, untie from the buoy, and sail away in our new ketch. You will be left here to build your house."

"Fair enough." Edwin looked down at the knot. "Then let's get to this."

The moment Joshua had finished tying the second constrictor knot, the anchor was released. Edwin took a large breath while he watched the coil unraveled, and then he was dragged down into the warm Caribbean water.

Joshua and Henry stood at the gunwale, each holding their breath as long as they could. After two minutes had passed, Henry let out his breath. "He's not coming up, Cap'n."

"No." Joshua let out his breath and shook his head.

"What were those two knots you tied?"

"They call them constrictor knots. They're special the millers use to tie the tops of the flour bags shut." Joshua looked at the sun. "Let's retrieve our anchor, cut Edwin's body loose, and get underway."

"Where are we going, Cap'n?"

"Kings Town, to find Long John Silver."

☠ ☠ ☠

Three days later, Joshua and Henry tied the *Seagull* up to the dock in front of Silver Jack's Tavern. After securing their new ketch to the rusty cleats, they walked across the dock, and pushed through the door into the public room.

John Silver stepped from the kitchen and spotted the two. "Welcome to Silver Jack's Tavern and Inn! I'm the proprietor, Jack Bridger."

Henry studied the old man for a moment and brightened. "I think I know you."

"Oh?"

"On Tortuga, just before I signed articles with you, a man who was missing his left leg sailed into Tortuga with a sea chest that looked to hold a treasure. He told me his name was Judas Pottersfield. Except for this man having two legs, fatter, and sportin' a beard, he's the spittin' image of that man."

Silver stepped to their table. "Welcome to Silver Jack's Tavern!" He pointed to the bay. "I see Edwin Drake made you the loan of his yacht."

"You know Edwin Drake?"

"I know everybody on Jamaica—some personally and the rest by reputation." He set two tankards on the table and filled them with ale. "Edwin was askin' around about a place where he could build himself a home, and I happened to know of some land out on the west tip of the island that would serve his purpose."

"Aye. We just now came—"

"Edwin was once my shipmate." Joshua gave Henry a kick under the table.

"Not many liked that man, so he's fortunate to have you as a mate." Jack rubbed his stomach. "When was the last time you two had a hot meal?"

"It's been a while." Joshua gave a sniff. "What can you offer us?"

"The misses just finished a pot of lamb stew that's fit for a king. What say I bring you two large bowls to go with that ale?"

Joshua nodded. "Yes, that would be good."

The moment Jack was gone, Joshua grabbed Henry's forearm and squeezed. "I don't want anybody knowing that we killed Edwin Drake."

"But the man needed killing, Cap'n, and you heard the innkeeper said about him. Not many liked Edwin."

"Jack Bridger knows Edwin, and we don't know who else in Kings Town knows him."

"Okay. Not a word to anybody that we did."

Silver returned with the food. "So, Edwin must have sent you here to buy building supplies."

"Aye, and some provisions too."

"Well, you've come to the right place because old Jack Bridger knows everybody in King's Town." He gave a raise of his bushy brows. "Show me your list and I'll tell you where to buy what you need."

"Actually, we're looking for a man named John Silver. Word in Savannah is that he's somewhere here in Jamaica."

Silver gave a laugh. "Long John Silver! Ha! I know the old pirate well!"

"How do we find him?"

"A secretive man if there ever was one." He studied the two with his sideways look. "And what—pray tell—would you need from the likes of that old pirate?"

"It's a personal matter."

"Suite yourselves." Silver gave a shrug, turned, and walked away toward the kitchen. "Personal matters best stay personal."

"Why didn't you tell him why you want to find John Silver, Cap'n?"

"I…" Joshua closed his eyes for a moment. "I didn't want to get into a long explanation about John Flint."

After a glass, Silver returned to the public room. After making the rounds with his pitcher of ale, he stepped to Joshua's and Henry's table and investigated their tankards. "More ale, mates?"

Henry reached with his foot and gave the old man's leg a kick. It was wood. "I was right! You're Cap'n Judas Pottersfield!"

"Who?"

"Judas Pottersfield." He pointed east. "Tortuga a few years back. You gave me my boat an' nearly slit me throat fer lookin' in yer sea chest."

Silver walked away and fetched a lantern. Upon his return, he held it close to Morgan's face. "Well, bend me to a yard if it isn't Henry Morgan, the Tortuga Crab Killer!"

"Then you remember me too."

"Aye, but I lied to ya, Henry. Judas Pottersfield was me incognito name, and all that bilge about being a famous pirate just for fun." Silver raised the light so he could see Joshua's face. "If what ye were sayin' back on Tortuga was true, this here must be that famous pirate you bragged about, Joshua Smoot, himself."

Henry gave Joshua a jab in the arm. "I told ya that you was famous, Cap'n."

"Is that right?" Silver held the lantern close to Smoot and moved it across so he could see the scar on Joshua's cheek. "Are you Joshua Smoot?"

"Aye."

"So, why do ya need this fellow—this Long John Silver?"

"Because I was told at Savannah that John Silver buried John Flint's body, and he's the only one who knows where."

"Then the rumor's correct. You are his bastard son!" He stepped back and hung the lantern on its hook. "You want to go pray o'er your dear departed father's bones." Jack gave a respectful nod. "I wish I had a son like you, even if he was a bastard."

Joshua shook his head. "It isn't for praying that I want to know where he's buried."

"Oh? Then why?"

"I want to dig up his body and throw it to the crabs on the Savannah mud flats."

"Why? What did Flint ever do to ya?"

"He killed my mother in front of me. He took me to England, and that ended up making me a slave on Cuba. He ruined my life. That's more than enough reason to hate John Flint."

"If I can get this John Silver fellow to agree to take you to John Flint's grave, what might ya be giving him in trade?"

"Trade?"

"Well, a man doesn't likely travel all the way from Kings Town to Savannah without some compensation, now does he?"

"He wouldn't need to go with us. He could give us a map."

"A map? Hmm."

"What would he want from Morgan and me?"

Silver looked at Joshua's right hand. "That's a nice ring ya be sportin' on yer finger. Can I have a look at it?"

Smoot started to pull it off but stopped. "Will it help you remember where Long John Silver might be?"

"Oh, I know where he is, Joshua. And I know how he thinks." He held out his hand.

"Here." Joshua handed him the ring.

"Nice." Silver rolled it around in his hand for a moment and then held it at arm's length. "These eyes aren't what they used to be. I'm gonna get my magnifier from the office." He went into his office and quickly heated some sealing wax. With a quick check that Smoot hadn't followed, he pressed the ring into the cooling wax and then returned to the public room with the magnifier.

"Much better." He stepped next to a lantern and studied the ring for a minute. "If this belonged to John Flint, John Silver might take it in exchange for a meeting."

"No—it was my mother's stick pin, and it's the only thing I have from her."

"A stick pin, you say?"

"A silversmith at Saint James Bay made it into a ring for me."

"Too bad it wasn't John Flint's ring." He handed it back to Joshua. "Long John Silver's a sentimental old pirate and would treasure a thing like that if it was."

"Would you talk to him for us?"

"Talk—yes—but I can't give any guarantee that he'll agree to anything."

"Do what you can, Mister Bridger. We'll be aboard the *Seagull* or about town."

"While you're about town, be sure to visit my brother's warehouses at the west end of the docks. He might have some of the building material that Edwin sent you here to buy."

☠ ☠ ☠

The next morning, Joshua and Henry walked west along the dock to the Noble Shipping Company where three merchantmen were loading and unloading cargo.

"Ahoy! Can I help you?" The man held a tablet and a pencil.

"I hope so." Joshua turned to the man. "It depends."

"It depends?" The man looked the two up and down. "You're obviously seafaring men, so that means you're either here to ask for employment, or to buy or sell something."

"We…"

Henry held up a hand. "Jack Bridger told us that Charles Noble is his brother and that we should meet him."

"So, it's just a social visit you're here about?"

"We need advice from Mister Noble about dealing with somebody he knows."

"Who might that somebody be?"

"A retired pirate named Long John Silver."

"So, you're on a quest."

"Is Mister Noble able to give us a few minutes of his time?"

"Stay here. I'll go see whether he's free." He stopped. "Do you have names?"

"I'm Joshua Smoot and this lad is Henry Morgan."

"Henry Morgan?" He stepped back to the lad. "Do you claim a relationship to our previous governor, or is your name a joke?"

"It's the name I chose for myself."

"He's an orphan." Joshua nodded toward the building. "It's of no concern."

"I'll be right back." The man was back in five minutes. "He'll see you, but he's a very busy man. Whatever it is you want to know about that old pirate, get straight to it."

"We will."

Charles Noble was sitting at a large desk covered with contracts and shipping manifests. He looked up. "Joshua Smoot and Henry Morgan." He stood and offered his hand. "My brother told me that you would be visiting me."

"Did he tell you who we were looking for?"

"Yes—the old pirate—Long John Silver." He pointed to two chairs. "Take a seat and tell me what you're willing to do for John Silver in exchange for a map to John Flint's grave." He set a bottle next to several glasses. "Can I offer you some of Jamaica's finest rum?"

"Yes!" Henry grabbed his glass and held it toward the bottle. "Two fingers if you will."

"Of course." He poured the liquor and capped the bottle. "If my memory is correct, it's Exodus 21:24 where Moses told the Hebrews to exact an eye for an eye and a tooth for a tooth but that was against a living person. Your father has been dead for several years. I don't see how scattering his bones on the mud flats of Savannah can possibly make up for him making you and your sister watch when he killed your mother."

"It isn't just killing her, because that set off a string of events that took my betrothed—Rebecca Keyes—from me. She forced her to exile me to a slave plantation at Baracoa."

"But you're now a free man. Why not expend this hatred in a more constructive way?"

"Such as?"

"Go find Rebecca and marry her."

"I've tried. She's gone."

After a long pause, Charles gave the two a smile. "My brother tells me that you are here in the *Seagull*—Edwin Drake's ketch."

"Edwin is dead." Henry turned and gave Joshua an impudent look. "He wasn't going to tell you, but you have to know."

"Well, I can't say the man will be missed." He offered more rum. "So, the ketch is now yours?"

"Yes." Joshua gave Henry a stern look. "It was Edwin and his father who sent me to Baracoa."

"I sold that yacht to Edwin, and regretted it the moment I took his money."

"We've taken up enough of your time, Mister Noble." Joshua stood and downed his rum. "If you are able to help us locate John Silver, then please send word to us. We are docked in front of your brother's tavern."

"I will do what I can."

It was during their third day at Silver Jack's that Charles Noble came looking for them. "Aboard the *Seagull*! It's me—Charles Noble! May I come aboard?"

"Aye!" Henry climbed up through the companionway while the man stepped across to the deck. "Did you talk with John Silver?"

"I spoke with him last evening."

"And?" Joshua pushed up past Henry. "Did he agree to talk to us?"

"No, but he agreed for me to be his intermediary."

"Did he tell you what he wants from us in exchange?"

"Yes. He asks that you do him a big favor."

"How big of a favor?"

"Let's go down to your cabin and I'll show you." Once settled, Charles pulled a folded chart from his pocket and spread it on the table. "Seems there's a small treasure on an island somewhere in the Antilles. He told me it isn't worth very much, but it has a special sentimental value to him."

"I don't know of any treasure on any island."

"Well, John Silver tells me that there's a man in New York Town who does."

"Since he knows who the man is, couldn't he go himself?"

"They had a falling out some years ago, but the Yorkman—Robert Ormerod—is like most businessmen."

"Meaning what?"

"John Silver knows that he will demand half of the treasure. You will carry a letter that guarantees that the treasure will be divided equally." Charles touched the bottom of the chart. "When he marks the treasure location, he must sign his name here at the bottom."

Joshua looked at Henry. "You'll do this with me?"

"It's a lot of work, but you're my captain."

Joshua turned back to Charles. "Tell John Silver that we'll do it—his map for our map."

"Good!" He pulled another piece of paper from his pocket. "His name is Robert Ormerod and this is his address." With that, Charles stood, climbed back up to the deck, jumped across to the dock and started away.

"What about provisions, Cap'n?"

"You're right. We're also running low on money." Joshua ran up onto the deck and called. "Mister Noble!"

The man stopped and turned. "Yes?"

"Since we'll be doing John Silver's bidding, would he be willing to give us the provisions we will need for the round trip?"

Charles considered for a moment. "I have a request, Joshua."

"Is it part of our agreement with John Silver?"

"A lot of seamen come to Silver Jack's Tavern with stories." Charles stepped toward Joshua and looked around to make sure nobody was listening. "I know about the agreement you've made with the merchants of Savannah, and I know that the British often block the river just as they did when your father was active."

"I know it's not a secret what my father did or what I have agreed to do for the merchants of Savannah." Joshua paused. "Where is this going?"

"Come with me." Charles turned and pointed west toward his warehouses. We can talk better over refreshments."

Ten minutes later, Charles poured three glasses of rum and pushed the two across to Joshua and Henry. "I want the *Seagull*, and I'm willing to trade you an armed topsail schooner for her."

"Cap'n!" Henry backed away to the door and waited for Joshua to follow. He leaned close and whispered. "We're pirates, Cap'n. Since you want to stop at Savannah to check on your windmill anyway, why don't we take us a prize or two so we have something to sell when we get there?"

"It would take a dozen crewmen to man such a ship. You and I can sail the *Seagull* to New York by ourselves. All we need is the food and some money."

"I can provide everything you will need, Joshua."

Joshua turned and looked at Charles. "You would do that for us?"

"Yes." Charles pointed at the chairs. "Please hear me out." The two took their seats. "I am a very rich businessman, and I didn't get rich by following every rule." He gave a wry smile. "Like the merchants of Savannah, I buy and sell both ships and their cargoes for a profit. There will come a day when you will want to bring one or more prize ships to Jamaica."

"I can see that, Mister Noble."

"I can't grant you a letter of marque because I am not the governor of a colony, but I can provide you with an armed ship and enough crewmen to do what Henry just suggested."

"How long will that take, sir?"

"Not long, Henry." Charles touched a sheet of paper covered with names. "I already have more than enough men who know who you two are and what you are about to do."

"John Silver wants a map and half of a treasure. What do you want, Mister Noble?"

"I want a partner in commerce like I had with your father. I want your word that any prize you cannot take into Savannah, you will bring to me."

"Show us the ship you'd trade for the *Seagull*."

After a short boat ride, the three boarded the sixty-foot armed sloop *Seacrest*. "She's quite a bit older than the *Seagull*, but my shipwright assures me that she is sound and has many more years on her keel."

"Six cannons." Henry jumped up onto the nearest one. "These are better than the ones we had on *El Pescador*, Cap'n!" He looked up at the mast and boom. "An' her sails look fresh."

"Her sails are the only thing that needed replacing." Charles pointed to the companionway. "Follow me."

After a thorough inspection of the crew quarters, the main cabin, and the kitchen, Joshua gave a nod. "I'll make it a point to bring you a prize every month, Mister Noble."

"Then we have a deal?"

"Yes."

"It will take me a few days to lay in the provisions and hire the crew you'll need."

"Henry and I will do whatever we can to help, sir."

That night back aboard the *Seagull*, Henry raised his glass of rum and gave a toast. "Here's to being back on the account!"

"Aye!" Joshua took a large gulp and lowered his glass. "But we must be careful, Henry."

"Why?"

"I have a feeling that there is something else going on here that Mister Noble isn't telling us."

"Even so, we're back in business, Cap'n."

"Aye, and like John Manley always told me back at Wakehurst, the smart man never looks a gift horse in the mouth."

A week later, as Joshua, Henry, and their crew of six sailed the sixty-foot armed sloop *Seacrest* up the Savannah River behind a prize ship, the red-sailed Virginia sharp-hulled *Remora* sailed north past Tybee Island with Long John Silver at the helm.

CHAPTER EIGHTEEN:
New York Mishap

*T*he pirate ship *Seacrest* pulled slowly past the barge that was driving the thirty-foot creosote-treated pilings deep into strata at the eastern side of Lamar's Creek. With each stroke of the huge machine, the black piling was driven another several inches into the riverbed.

While the crew threw their lines across to the men on the western dock, a man called stepped past the bales and barrels. "Hello! Is Captain Smoot about!"

Joshua walked across the deck and looked down on the Dutchman. "Willem! I was just marveling at how much you've accomplished in such a short time!" He spread his arms. "This is incredible!"

"Yes, it is my friend, and I'm here to give you the grand tour of your new industry!"

"Aye! Give me a moment to confer with the crew, and I'll be right there!" Ten minutes later, Joshua stepped from the gangway onto the partially-finished dock.

"With the dredging complete, we began driving the pilings down into the river bottom the day you left for New York." He turned and pointed.

"I've taken the liberty to arrange your various industries in such a way that they will best serve the ships and wagons that will pay for the use of your mill." He pointed south, toward the rice fields. "That brick building is going to be an iron foundry." He pointed west to the framed buildings. "Those two will be cotton presses, and this closest one will be where grain is received and the ground flower is stored until it is sold."

"What about the saw mill and where the logs and the finished lumber will be stored?"

Willem pointed east, past the windmill. "That will be done on the east side of the creek once the pilings are in place and the other dock is built." He looked to the *Seacrest*. "Have you brought more cargo to sell to Savannah?"

"Yes—a hold full of cargo that should cover the rest of what I owe you."

"I trust you for the money, Joshua." He pointed at the windmill. "So, is this what you imagined it would look like?"

"Oh, much more than I imagined." He made a quick survey of the workmen that surrounded the structure. "Did the Archimedes Screws and the special gearing arrive yet?"

"Yes, but they're at my yards for now."

"When will the windmill begin turning?"

"Three weeks—a month at the most." He pointed at the barge that was driving the pilings into the river. "The docks will be finished by then, and we'll be ready to start milling lumber and grain."

"Wonderful!" Joshua looked to the *Seacrest*. "If you don't mind, I'm going to see to the selling of our prize and cargoes up at the old cotton docks."

Two days later, the prize ship and its cargo had been sold, and Willem Kesteren was paid for the work at Lamar's Creek. After another visit with his sister Sarah, Joshua cast off the Lamar Creek docks and set sail for New York City.

☠ ☠ ☠

The *Seacrest* arrived at New York Town three days after John Silver and the *Remora*. At Charles Noble's suggestion, Henry played the part of a courier to hand deliver the letter of introduction requesting Joshua's meeting with Robert Ormerod.

Henry knocked at the door and stepped back down onto the sidewalk.

Robert opened the door and looked down at the lad. "Yes?"

"Are you…" Henry turned the note around. "Are you Robert Ormerod?"

"Yes. Is that a message for me?"

"Yes, sir." He stepped back up the steps and handed the man the note. Robert pulled a coin from his pocket and held it out. "Uh…I was told to wait for an answer."

Robert broke the wax seal and read quickly. "Who is John Manley?"

"I'm only a messenger, sir. Like I said, he paid me to deliver that note and bring back your answer."

"He didn't tell you anything about himself or why he wanted to meet with me?"

"I'd tell you if I knew, sir."

Robert looked at his pocket watch. "It's ten o'clock. You may tell John Manley that I will see him lunch."

"What time would that be, sir?"

"Two o'clock. Tell Mister Manley to be here at two o'clock."

Henry ran the mile back to the dock and called out as he approached the ship. "I'm back, Cap'n!"

Joshua stepped to the rail and called. "What did he say?"

"Two o'clock, Cap'n!"

"After he read the note, did he ask you any questions about me?"

"I told him I was just a messenger, and that I didn't know anything about you."

"Well, everything is going as planned."

Joshua arrived at precisely two o'clock and rapped three times on the Ormerod front door. While he waited, he made a final inspection of his wardrobe and hair.

The door opened. "John Manley?"

"Yes." Joshua stepped back and gave a curt bow. "Thank you for seeing me on such short notice."

"Come inside, John." Robert ushered Joshua to the parlor and offered him a drink. "The note said that you have come from Savannah about an important business matter."

"Yes." Joshua opened his leather valise, pulled out the map Charles had given him, and spread it on the table. "I have been told by my employer that you hid something on an island off the north coast of Saint Croix some years ago. He said that it contained something of personal value to him, and is willing to pay you one hundred dollars for its location and signature on this map."

"Who are you working for?" Robert put the stopper back in the bottle. "It's an old man with a wooden left leg, isn't it?"

"I'm…" Joshua shook his head and put a hand on the map. "He sent me—"

"I'm right, aren't I!" Robert reached into a desk drawer and picked up a pistol. "You are a foot soldier of Long John Silver, the shipmate of John Flint." He pointed the pistol at Joshua.

"If you will simply mark the location and sign your name—"

"Out!" Robert pulled back the hammer. "Get out of my house!"

As Joshua stepped out onto the stoop, a young woman pushed a perambulator toward the steps. The toddler at her hand let go, scrambled up the stairs and hugged her father's leg. "Daddy! Daddy!"

"Hi, Honey." He put the pistol behind his back. "Did you have fun at the park?"

"Oh, yes!" She turned and looked back at her nanny. "Clara and I fed the ducks, Daddy! They ate all the bread that mommy sent, and they want more!"

"Well, Jane, that's the best news I've heard all day."

"Look, Daddy." She held up a finger. "One of the white ducks tried to eat my finger, but I wouldn't let him."

"Here." Robert swept Jane up into his arms. "Let me kiss it all better."

The nanny pushed the perambulator to the steps. "She wants to go back to the park tomorrow, sir. Would you mind?"

"Not at all, and there is always leftover bread at the bakeries we can have for pennies." He gave the nanny a smile and kissed Jane on the cheek. "Have you named any of the ducks yet?"

"No, but I think I'll name the one that bit me, Nipper."

Robert noticed that Joshua was still there. "Clara. Take Jane to her mother." Once the two were gone, Robert turned back to Joshua, and pointed the pistol at his heart. "The next time I see you, Mister Manley, I will shoot you."

Ten minutes later, Joshua walked into the King's Domain Tavern, stood for a moment to allow his eyes accommodated to the darkness.

"Over here, Cap'n!" Henry signaled to a waitress for another ale. "That didn't go well, did it?"

"You saw that?"

"Aye. I watched the whole thing."

"He accused me of being John Silver's agent and threatened to kill me if I ever showed my face again." The ale came and he took a large drink. "I'm sorry I brought you and the others all the way to New York for nothing."

"Those men have been well rewarded, Cap'n. They got their shares of the prize we sold at Savannah, and those who came for the ride home thanked me and left."

"I don't understand Charles Noble or John Silver." He shook his head. "They both knew we would fail."

"But we haven't failed yet, Cap'n."

"You saw him, Henry. Nothing is going to change that man's mind."

"Didn't nobody ever teach you about leverage, Cap'n—the kind of leverage that will get you your map, all signed and sealed?"

"I know about using leverage, Henry, but we don't have any."

"Mister and Misses Ormerod have something much more important to them than any treasure."

"Go on."

"Their little girl—Jane." Henry leaned close. "Those two know John Silver's reputation, and would give their souls to protect that little girl from him." He reached across and touched the map. "A mark on that map is nothing compared to losing their child to a blood-thirsty pirate."

"We don't hurt children."

"We won't hurt the little girl, Cap'n, but that's how these things are done. We take the girl to someplace secret and safe and hold her for ransom." Henry gave a toothy smile. "Then it's back to Kings Town where you trade the map for where John Flint is buried."

"Someplace secret and safe?"

"I spotted an empty sail loft near where we docked the *Seacrest*. It's a perfect place to keep the toddler while you deal with her mother and father."

"But there's a problem. We don't know when or where to abduct the little girl."

"Oh?" Henry took another gulp of ale. "I saw you and Ormerod arguing on the porch, and I saw the nanny bringing the girl home." He gave a wink. "I'd wager that those two will be feeding ducks at that same park again tomorrow afternoon."

Joshua raised his glass. "Let's finish our ale and go find those hungry ducks." A half hour later, the two pirates stood watching several children throwing bread scraps out into the pond. "This is perfect." He turned to Henry. "Show me the sail loft."

As expected, the nanny pushed the perambulator out the front door of the Ormerod home just after noon with the little girl walking at her side. Jane carried a sack filled with bread.

"Are you sure you don't want to put that in the buggy?"

"No, Clara. Daddy said I'm a big enough girl to carry this."

"Well, if you get tired, we can always give the bread a ride."

"Can we give the duckies a ride too?"

Clara gave a friendly laugh. "Sure, Jane, if you can get them to jump in, we'll give them a ride all the way around the park."

Joshua watched the two as they approached the pond. "She hasn't taken her eyes off the little girl for a moment." He turned to Henry. "It's time for that diversion."

"I like to fight." He pointed at two young lovers sitting on a bench across the walkway from the pond. "So, I'm going to do to that young man what Edwin Drake did to you."

Within five minutes, Henry and the young man were trading punches, swearing at each other, and rolling on the grass. People from all over the park rushed to the two. The nanny stayed near Jane and the ducks but turned her back just long enough for Joshua to grab the girl and drop the ransom note in the perambulator. In a moment, the two were gone.

It took Henry a half hour to reach the sail loft. His knuckles were bloody and his face was bruised. "You got her Cap'n!"

"Aye, and you took a beating to make it happen." He gave the lad a nod. "I'll remember that."

"Ah, this is nothing. You should see me after a real fight." He followed Joshua into the sail loft and looked at the girl. Her face was smeared from tears. "Is she alright?"

"Yes—just tears." Joshua walked to the door and held up the map. "This shouldn't take very long."

"How will I know when to bring her to you?"

"I'll have Ormerod send one of his footmen to tell you."

"Wait, Cap'n!" Henry followed to the loft door. "That won't work."

"Why not?"

"You can't tell him or his footman where I'm holding her, and we both have to be long gone before they get her back." He pointed at the toddler. "The moment Ormerod has her, he'll hunt us down and kill us."

"Then..?"

"We have to…" Henry looked toward the *Seacrest*. "Once you have his mark and his signature on the map, tell him to send his footman here with a white flag." He pointed. "Have him tie it to that third cleat and then go away. Tell him that I will be watching from a distance, and when I see it, I'll send the girl home in a cab."

"I can see that you've been in this business longer than me, Henry." With that, Joshua turned and walked away.

☠ ☠ ☠

John Silver watched and listened to everything that occurred between Robert, Joshua, and Henry. He stepped back from his vantage point, turned, and walked away into town. He stopped at a building with a sign that read, DOWELL & SONS MORTUARY.

John Silver stepped inside and recoiled at the smell of chemicals and death.

"May I help you?" The man was tall, slender, and very pale. "Are you looking for a departed family member?"

"Yes—my granddaughter."

"Why would you believe that she is here?"

"I don't believe it, but the family has searched for two days and my hope has turned to despair."

"There are several children in our morgue. What is your granddaughter's age?"

"She's four." Silver pretended to cry. "They are blaming me, and I suppose that they are right."

"Oh?"

"I asked them if I could take her to the park for the afternoon, and they agreed. But when we got there, an old shipmate got me into a conversation."

"So, she wandered off while you were supposed to be watching her?"

"I'm trying to find her, and I'm praying that she is not here."

The man took a large breath and let it out slowly.

"I have three small girls for you to see." He pointed to a doorway. 'If one of them is your granddaughter, you can take her."

"Thank you for being so understanding." Silver followed the man to a room with several dozen bodies arranged in rows by age.

"Actually, none of these bodies have been identified, so if your little girl is here, then that's one body that I won't have to put in a pauper's grave." The mortician pulled back the three sheets to expose the small girls. "Well?"

"Oh, Lord!" He pointed to the one who looked most like Jane Ormerod. "That's Elizabeth!" He put a hand on the girl and pretended to sob.

"Uh, I hate to sound like a mercenary, but there is a fee that I am required to charge you for taking her." The man went to a cabinet and brought back a clean sheet. "It's five dollars."

"Here." John Silver handed the man the five coins and waited while the body was wrapped.

"Thank you." Silver took the body to the room he had rented and laid her on the bed next to a new child's dress. Then he went to the docks where a young prostitute was waiting.

"I just about gave up on you, Mister." She was in her late teens—a little older than Henry. "What took you so long?"

"I told you it would take me a while, and I paid you well to wait."

"Yes, you did." She put her hand on his arm. "Do you have a place for us to go?"

"I haven't hired you for my sake."

"Oh?" She let go of his arm. "Look, Mister, I don't want any trouble."

"Don't worry. My grandson is waiting for me at an abandoned sail loft down at the docks. He has never been with a woman, and since he is turning fourteen and has never been with a woman, my present to him is you."

"Then..?" She gave a laugh. "This sounds like fun."

"I've rented a room for the night at that inn across the dock. He knows that I am bringing him a special present, but he doesn't know what it is yet."

"What if he asks me who is paying for this? What do I tell him?"

"Tell him it's his best friend."

"Okay." She gave a giggle and pushed up her breasts. "Lead the way."

Silver led her south toward Cragen's Dock and pointed at the sail loft. "He's waiting inside."

"Here goes." She walked to the door, knocked lightly, and called. "Henry?"

Henry came to the door and peeked between the boards. "Who is it?"

"My name is Daisy, and your best friend sent me to you as a present. He's paid for me, for a room, and he gave me a bottle of rum for us to share."

Henry opened the door and looked at the young girl. "Aye, ye're a pretty one." He looked back to where Jane was asleep behind a stack of canvas. "You say you have a room, and my friend sent you?"

"Yes." She pointed at the inn across the dock from the *Seacrest*. "The rum is waiting."

"Uh…" He looked back at Jane again.

"You do like girls, don't you?"

"Of course, I do." He hesitated. "I can't be gone long, so if we're going to do this, let's hurry." Henry shut the loft door and pushed a rock up against the door.

"Catch me!" With a giggle, Daisy skipped ahead and spun around. As he followed, she kept just out of reach until they reached the inn.

Henry and the prostitute had been gone for only five minutes when John Silver carried the corpse of the four-year-old girl into the sail loft. He set the body behind a stack of canvas, stepped around to the small girl, and removed her gag. "Jane, are you alright?"

"Are you another bad man?"

"Oh, no!" He bent down, untied her hands and feet, and brushed the dirt from her dress. "I'm an old friend of your father. I'm here to take you home."

"Okay." She rubbed her wrists. "Can we go now?"

"Of course, we can, but I have a large bag of bread outside that I was wondering…"

"The ducks!" She jumped up and down. "Can we go feed the ducks first?"

"Yes, but your mother told me that she has a birthday dress she wants you to try on." He held out the dress to her. "It's prettier than the dirty one you are wearing."

"Okay." It took her only a moment. "Here's my old dress."

"Good girl." He led her outside to the bag of bread. "You hold the bag of bread while I go back and make sure I didn't forget anything inside."

"Okay." She took hold of the bag. "My name is Jane. What's your name?"

"John Silver." It took only a moment to put the dress onto the dead girl, lay her where Jane was lying, and tie the ropes around her hands and feet. With a final look to make sure everything was as it should be, he picked up Henry's lamp and set the straw and wood shavings ablaze.

☠ ☠ ☠

Robert was furious and held the cocked pistol at Joshua's forehead. "Tell me where my daughter is or I'll kill you right now!"

"And then what?"

"What do you mean?"

"Your daughter is alive and well, Mister Ormerod. She is being held in a safe place, and when he sees the white flag, he will know that you have signed and marked the map. Once your footman is gone, Henry will hire a cab and send Jane home to you."

"You'll get your map when I have Jane safe in my arms!"

"Please, Robert!" It was Moira. "We have to do it the way Mister Manley says we must."

"But…" Robert looked at the clock. "Three hours! You've had her for three hours!"

"And as God is my witness, you'll have her within an hour after I leave with the map."

"Very well." Robert signed his name and wrote the date on the map. As his ink pen hovered over the island, he stopped and looked up at Joshua. "I'll not mark the location of the treasure until Jane is safely back in my arms."

"Then we are at—"

Before he finished the words, there was a commotion outside. The three rushed to the front stoop where Henry Morgan stood in the middle of the street with a charred body at his feet. Before they could move, Henry cried out. "I didn't do it! I was only gone for a few minutes! When I came back, the lamp was tipped over and everything was on fire.!"

Moira pushed past Robert and Joshua, ran down the stairs and fell to her knees on the cobblestones. "Please God! No!"

Henry backed away several steps and yelled. "Run, Joshua! Run for your life!"

While Robert joined Moira, Joshua and Henry ran through the crowd—one to the east and the other to the west. "Damn you two!" Robert pulled out his two pistols and fired one at each of them. "They've killed her! They've burned our Jane to death!"

With the signed map in hand, Joshua ran back to their schooner. He stopped at the gangway, turned, and searched the streets for Morgan.

"Cap'n?" The lad peeked from behind a tree thirty paces away. "I…"

"Damn you, Henry Morgan!" He pulled his pistol, cocked it, and fired at the boy. "You'll die for what you did this day!"

☠ ☠ ☠

John Silver stood behind Jane as she threw her last scraps of bread to the white ducks. She turned to the old man. "It's all gone, Mister Silver. Can you take me home now?"

"I think that would be a wonderful idea, but before we go, I have something for you to give to your mother and father. He pulled a sealed letter from his pocket, placed it in her hand. "Now, let's go see your mommy and daddy."

As the two rounded the last corner, John Silver stopped, put his foot up on a flower pot, and pretended to adjust his stocking. "You run ahead, Jane. I'll be right there."

"Okay!" Jane turned and ran to her home. Once on the porch, she tried the latch, but it was locked. "Mommy? Daddy?" As the door pulled open, she held up the letter. "Mister Silver gave me this letter for you to read!"

The two gasped and fell to their knees. "Oh, merciful God in heaven! The Lord's answered our prayers!"

As Moira showered her daughter with kisses, Robert opened the letter and scanned it quickly. "Moira!"

"What?"

"The letter. Listen." He looked down and read. "Robert and Moira: Here is your precious daughter, Jane, safe and sound. I had nothing to do with the kidnapping, but I did send Joshua Smoot and Henry Morgan to New York to ask you to mark the location of Captain Rip Rap's treasure. I followed them to make sure they would do as I said, but when they took Jane hostage, I had to get involved. I went to the morgue and bought the body of a little girl that was Jane's size, switched her for Jane, and set the fire to the sail loft while Henry was away with a prostitute.

I may be a black-hearted pirate, but I have never killed a woman or a child, and every man that I've have killed deserved it. Oh, and I swear that I will someday have the treasure of Dead Man's Chest, with or without your help. Long John Silver."

"Long John Silver did this to us?"

"Yes." Robert nodded. "I'd kill him for it but—"

"No, Robert. He saved our little girl."

☠ ☠ ☠

Two weeks later, the *Seacrest* docked in front of Silver Jack's Tavern. Most of the crew were new men who had joined the crew for working passage south. Joshua walked straight to the Noble Warehouse and to the office of Charles Noble.

"Joshua!" Charles stood and offered his hand. "Did you get it?"

"Of course, I did."

Charles looked at the leather satchel. "May I see it?"

"Yes, but not until I get what I want from John Silver."

"Of course." Charles pulled a folded and sealed letter from a drawer and set it on his desk. "There. Now may I have the map?"

Joshua placed the folded map next to the letter. "There—signed and sealed."

Charles studied the map and the signature. "Did he ask who sent you?"

"Yes. He wanted to know if it was Long John Silver...the one-legged pirate."

"What did you tell him?"

"What you told me to say—that the map was for the anonymous investor in Savannah."

Charles pulled out a piece of parchment and compared signatures. The signatures matched. "Good. This is Robert Ormerod's hand." He looked up at Joshua. "Where's your lap dog—Henry Morgan?"

"I left him in New York Town."

"You two had a falling out?"

"We kidnapped Ormerod's little girl and I left Morgan to watch her."

"What happened?"

"There was a fire. The little girl was killed." Joshua shook his head. "Robert tried to kill us, but I ran one way and Henry ran the other."

"I'm so sorry, Joshua. Nobody was supposed to get hurt."

"Henry Morgan will." He put his hand on his pistol. "He'll pay with his life for killing the little girl."

A week later, Joshua sailed the *Seacrest* up the Savannah River to the cotton docks where he sold a prize ship and its cargo to the merchants of the town. Using the map Charles Noble gave him, he took two of his men to Flint's Bluff at the eastern cliffs that overlooked the new windmill, docks, and warehouses. The body was exactly where John Silver's map said it would be. While he watched, his two crewmen exhumed the body.

"What now, Captain?"

"I want it taken to down to the flats just east of my new docks." He gave the sail-wrapped body a kick. "Load it in the wagon and let's be about this."

Twenty minutes later, John Flint's body was dropped unceremoniously onto the dirt. One of the men pulled his knife, and starting at the feet, cut the canvas, and spread it apart to expose the mummified body. He looked up at Joshua. "What now, Captain?"

"That's enough. You two can go back to the ship now." While the two retreated, Joshua dragged the body across to the mud-bound wreckage of the Walrus and gave it a vicious kick. The head and an arm broke loose from the rotted canvas, and with several more well-placed kicks, the rest of the body broke up into separate parts. "There, just as I promised." He looked about at several carrion birds. "Now I will let the birds and crabs pick your bones clean."

It took the birds and the crabs just two weeks to strip the bones clean. When Joshua was finally satisfied with his revenge, he gathered the bones, piled them together on the deck, doused John Flint's old ship with whale oil, and set it ablaze.

He stood on the bluff to the west for most of the day while the old ship burned down to the mud. With his revenge complete and the construction of the windmill and the docks well underway, he gathered a small crew, boarded his topsail schooner, and set sail for the open seas.

CHAPTER NINETEEN:
The Cannons of Amazing Grace

*T*he Port of Falkirk played a pivotal role from the time of the Romans to the present. Situated on the east coast of central Scotland, the town lay near the cities of Edinburgh and Glasgow—a natural magnet for the farmers and factories to congregate to sell their livestock, wool, and cottage-made wares. With the shift from agriculture to industry in the mid-eighteenth century, Falkirk became the center of manufacturing. Among the many textile mills and iron foundries was the Carron Iron Works where Charles Gascoigne invented a new kind of cannon.

The British Navy bought over a thousand of the new carronades in varying bore sizes, but due to several accidents that killed naval gunners, the British Navy decided they did not like the carronades and delivered them back to the Carron Company warehouse at the Falkirk docks. There was nothing wrong with the cannons. The problem was that the gunners did not follow the new procedures, and rather than find out what was wrong, the Navy instructed all ships to replace the carronades with the older reliable weapons. Therefore, the one-thousand carronades sat for months in the Carron Company warehouse.

When the letter reached the founding fathers informing them of the cannons, George Washington dispatched the merchant ship *Amazing Grace* with privateer captain David Hayward in command. He also sent his adjunct, Joseph Reed to Falkirk with sufficient funds to buy the cannons.

Charles Gascoigne, the manager of the Carron Iron Works met the ship. "Welcome to Falkirk, gentlemen. May I come aboard?"

Captain Hayward escorted the Scotsman to his cabin where Joseph Reed was waiting. "May I offer you a Cuban cigar and a glass of Port wine while we discuss the cannons?"

"Yes—that would be wonderful." He held up the cigar. "But my wife must not know that I indulged."

"If she asks, I will tell her that the smell on your coat is from our cigars."

"Then let us begin with a toast." Charles raised his glass. "Here's to the Americans, that the thousand carronades that the British Navy rejected will come back to haunt them!"

"Here, here!" Joseph took a sip of his wine and set down his goblet. "Correct me if I am wrong, Charles, but General Washington told me that the British never demanded that their money for the cannons be returned."

"Your general is correct, and therefore, you need not pay me for the cannons." He took a moment to bite off the two ends of the cigar, light it, and took several welcome puffs. "Call it my contribution to the liberation of the American Colonies from the oppressing English."

"But there must be—"

"I will allow you to pay for the standard package of shot and powder for each cannon, but like I told General Washington in my initial dispatch, the British Navy already compensated us for these cannons."

"What happened? Why did they bring them back?"

"As you know, the carronade is a third the weight of the standard long guns. The Brits figured they could carry three times the cannons by switching. But when they came up against the Americans—who were still using long guns—the shorter range of the carronades became a problem."

"Let me guess." Captain Hayward refilled the man's goblet. "They tried to compensate by using too much gunpowder."

"Yes, and America is the beneficiary of that poor decision." Charles turned to Joseph. "I have a nagging question, Mister Reed."

"I would you to have several questions."

"You know of course that there is a British blockade at most of the American ports where a cargo such as this could be smuggled to your military forces."

"Yes—and there are also foreign privateers and pirates foraging for anything that can be sold or traded for gold."

"I know that the cannons will be used as ballast and covered with a thin layer of stones, but the British are not stupid. They will not be fooled by your cargo of textiles."

"General Washington and the other investors have a plan." He turned to Captain Hayward. "Since you will be doing it, you can explain it to him."

"What kind of plan?" Charles looked to David. "How can you prevent the British from looking for something smuggled in the ballast?"

"Once *Amazing Grace* is far at sea, I will have several pigs slaughtered. Their body parts will be arranged to resemble two human beings, and then they will be sewn up into sail cloth."

"Oh?"

"Like you correctly pointed out, there's a good chance that a British man-of-war, a pirate, or an enemy privateer will decide to take *Amazing Grace* as a prize."

"Go on."

"If we are boarded by one of those three, we will claim that a disease—possible typhoid—is aboard and has killed half the crew. The two rotting bags of pig flesh will stink and turn them away."

"I understand about the typhoid, but what I don't understand is how you, Captain Hayward, will explain why you've kept two bodies aboard when all the other dead have been buried at sea."

"It's the Baptist preacher, Ezekiel McClanahan."

"The Baptist preacher?" He gave a wry smile. "How did you convince a Scottish minister of the Gospel to be a part of such a lie?"

"Two things. Ezekiel has a son in Virginia, and several other family members who are fighting for their religious liberty. His agreement to be a part of the deception has earned him free passage to the colonies."

"So, he...?"

"He's thought this out, and after much prayer, he has come to the conclusion that God wants those cannons to reach America."

"Well, we can only hope and pray that your voyage will take you directly to Virginia and to General Washington."

"There's one other thing you didn't tell him, Captain Hayward."

"That's right." David put his hand on Joseph's shoulder. "Mister Reed will be going along and posing as a common seaman. If—God forbid—we are taken by pirates or privateers, Joseph will volunteer to help sail *Amazing Grace* to where it will be sold."

"And if it is the British?"

"Then Providence—our God in heaven—will decide the outcome."

The loading of the carronades and the supporting equipment took three days and nights to accomplish. At dawn of the fourth day, *Amazing Grace* set sail for America.

☠ ☠ ☠

The *Seacrest* had been at sea for two weeks when the topman spotted the merchantman *Amazing Grace*. "On deck! Merchantman ten miles, two points on the starboard bow!"

Joshua came from his cabin, climbed to the quarterdeck, and shaded his eyes.

"There, Cap'n!" The man at the wheel pointed. "You can just now see her top-gallants."

Joshua took the spyglass from the binnacle and studied the ship. "A merchantman flying a Scottish flag." He closed the glass. "It won't be Spanish gold, but I've had good luck with Scottish ships in the past."

"The crew have their hearts set on gold, Cap'n."

"I know, but it won't hurt to stop the Scots to see what they carry."

Two hours later, *Amazing Grace* heaved to and watched as twenty pirates rowed across from the *Seacrest*. Once on deck, Joshua demanded that the captain present himself.

"I'm David Hayward—captain of the merchantman *Amazing Grace*."

Joshua made a quick count of the men assembled behind the captain. "Only seven of you?"

Hayward gave a nod. "We left Falkirk with three officers, a bosun, and twelve crewmen."

"Sixteen left Scotland and nine are gone? What happened to those other men?"

"As best as I can tell, it began with typhoid and then the cholera added itself to the killing of my crew."

Joshua gave a slight gasp. "When did the last man die?"

"Last night. He had been sick for the whole day and succumbed just after sunset. We put his body over the side this morning."

"So..?"

"Yes. The disease is still killing us as we speak."

"I have seen cholera at work. Your food and water are contaminated." Joshua backed away a step.

"We've thrown the water we were drinking over the side, and nobody has eaten anything for three days."

"What are you carrying, and where are you taking it?"

"Machines from the iron works at Falkirk mostly."

"What kind of machines?"

"Weaving machines, printing presses, farm plows, and several hundred iron cooking pots. We are also carrying several thousand bolts of cloth, flatware, and other homemaking items."

"Cap'n Smoot!"

"Not yet, Lukas." Joshua turned back to the captain, but the man was insistent.

"It's important that you know what we found, Cap'n!"

"I know about the cargo. Captain Hayward just told me."

"It's something else, Cap'n—something bad that may change everything."

"What is it?"

"While Jacob an' me were making the inventory, we went down to the bilges."

"Get to it, Lukas. What did you find that is so important?"

"When we got down to the bilges there was a god-awful stink."

"Bilges always stink, Lukas."

"There's two dead bodies sewn up in sailcloth, and they're juices are seeping through the canvas onto the ballast stones."

Smoot turned to Captain Hayward. "Explain!"

"Those two died four days ago."

"Why have you kept two of the dead aboard instead of putting them over the side with the others?"

"The Scottish preacher did that."

"What preacher?"

"He's in his cabin."

Smoot looked aft to the officer's country. "I'll be in the master's cabin." He pointed at Captain Hayward. Send that preacher to me!"

"We're a dying crew, Captain Smoot. If you care for your life and the lives of your men, you'll go away and leave us to face our fate."

"Your ship and the cargo it's carrying will not die of cholera. It belongs to me now, and I will sell them both to the merchants of Savannah." Smoot strode to the companionway, stopped, and turned. "The preacher! Bring him to me!"

By the time the old man knocked at the door, Smoot had lit a cigar and poured himself a glass of Scotch whiskey. "Come!"

"You called for me?"

"Yes!" Smoot pointed at the single chair across the table. "Sit down." He held up the cigar and tapped the goblet. "Do you smoke? Do you imbibe?"

"Neither."

"But I know for a fact that there's no mention in the Bible of tobacco, and your Savior turned water into wine at the Cana wedding." Smoot gave the old man a condescending grin. "We all have our beliefs, but it is the prudent man who bases those beliefs on the facts of scripture rather than tradition."

"You're correct about tobacco and wine, sir, but we Scottish Baptists abstain from those things to set a good example for our congregation."

"It's just you and me, and I don't need your good example." The little preacher shook his head. "Well then, all I can offer you is some of your captain's water."

"Yes—water would be good—as long as it is clean."

"My name is Joshua Smoot." He filled the second goblet with water and pushed it forward several inches. "What is your purpose aboard a merchantman full of machinery, home goods, and textiles?"

"My name is Ezekiel McClanahan. My eldest son William is in Culpeper Virginia with several other preachers trying to establish Baptist churches. When his mother died, I decided to join William in that place to help him with his ministry."

"Tell me, Ezekiel, about the two bodies in the bilges. The captain said that the two have been dead four days and you are to blame for them still being aboard."

"The twins." The old man gave a huff. "Matthew and Mark McTavish were in my congregation at Glasgow. Their family immigrated to America two years ago, and it was time for the twins to join them. They didn't have the money to buy passage, so they signed on as crewmen. Everything was fine until the crew started getting sick. The twins begged me that if they should die, I would deliver their bodies to their family in Virginia."

"Are you telling me that a preacher's promise to a couple of lowly deck hands—"

"Captain Hayward and I both swore it to the twins."

"So here I am, the new owner of *Amazing Grace*—a prize ship and its cargo that will be worth thousands to the merchants of Savannah—and I have two rotting bodies in the bilges that you insist must be delivered to their family in Virginia?" He dropped the stub of his cigar into his empty goblet. "Pretend for a moment that you are me—a pirate who has a crew hungry for the gold this ship and its cargo will bring you. What would you do with those two bodies?"

"If I were you—and the good Lord knows I would never wish to be a pirate—I would take my men off this death ship before they also catch this deadly disease. Then I would sail away, thank the good Lord for sparing me, and look for a better prize."

"The way I see it, as long as nobody goes down near those two bodies, nobody else will get the disease."

"If you take this ship to Savannah, you'll spread the disease."

"That's my concern, not yours."

"What about us—the remaining crew and me?"

"You'll be delivered and released at the docks at Savannah to fend for yourselves."

"Then the bodies of Matthew and Mark will remain aboard and I can take them to their families in Virginia?"

"Yes, but since none of my men will go near the rotting bodies, you will be responsible for their removal and transportation from Savannah."

"Thank you, Captain Smoot." The preacher stood. "Is that all?"

"No." He pointed at the chair. "Sit back down."

"What else have I done?"

"Since you're a man of God, I have a religious question for you."

"Yes?"

"I killed three men recently out of revenge for what they did to me. Will God forgive me for those two sins?"

"No—God requires the death of the sinner."

"But…" Smoot sat back and thought for a moment. "I was under the impression that he is a forgiving God. What if I repent, ask him to forgive me, and promise to never kill again?"

"You are not going to like what I'm about to tell you, Captain Smoot, but it is God's truth."

"Tell me, and let me be the judge of that."

"God never has and never will forgive a man's sin."

"If you believe that, then you are not a man of God." Smoot pulled his pistol from his sash and laid it on the table between them. "I would judge that you are around seventy years old. If you wish to live another day—"

"Hear me out, Captain Smoot, because what I have to say bears directly upon your question regarding the three men you killed."

Smoot touched the pistol. "Then get to your point quickly."

"If a man owes you money and satisfies that debt when he is supposed to, must you also forgive that debt?"

"I…" It took Smoot a moment. "No. I would take the money and declare his debt paid. A debt that is satisfied does not need to be forgiven."

"Why not?"

"Because forgiveness of a debt and the satisfaction of that same debt are contrary to one another."

"And what if another person stepped forward and satisfied that man's debt?"

"The debt would be satisfied, just as if the man had paid it himself."

"Would you need to tell the man or his benefactor that you have forgiven that debt?"

"No—it no longer needs forgiving."

"God declares over and over that the only way that the wages of a man's sin is satisfied is by the sinner's death and his eternal separation from God in the lake of fire."

"So, you're telling me that everybody must pay their own sin debt by going to hell—that God doesn't forgive our sins when we ask Him to?"

"I told you that you would not like it."

"This goes against everything I have ever heard."

"If we could get God's forgiveness of our sins by doing something like repenting, confessing, promising to do better in the future, then Jesus did not have to die on that Roman cross nearly fourteen-hundred years ago."

"Wait!" Smoot looked down at the pistol for several breaths. "Are you saying that Jesus' death on the cross did something other than make forgiveness possible for the churched?"

"Tradition and man's sinfulness have confused forgiveness of sin with salvation. The two are not the same."

"Then answer my question. Who goes to heaven?"

"Saved people go to heaven and unsaved people go to hell."

"Then how does an unsaved person get saved?"

"It's John 1:29 and 3:16. Salvation comes by believing who Jesus is and what He accomplished for mankind on that Roman cross fourteen-hundred years ago."

"Who is Jesus?"

"He is Emanuel—God in the flesh."

"Okay." Joshua touched his pistol. "What must I believe that Jesus accomplished on the cross?"

"Not that He paid the price or forgave our sins, but rather that He took away our sins to never hold them against us again." Ezekiel stood. "That is the good news—the Gospel of Grace."

"Enough." Smoot pointed at the cabin door. "Leave me."

CHAPTER TWENTY:
The French Corvette Le Tiburon

*T*he *Seacrest* and *Amazing Grace* sailed in tandem for Savannah, and just after noon of the third day, the top watch called down with an urgent message.

"On deck! Land ho!"

"Aye!" Smoot shaded his eyes against the sun and called back. "And what of the British?"

"There's two of them, Cap'n, an' they're both running free."

"Damn!" Smoot turned to Captain Hayward. "You heard!"

"Yes." He looked toward the west. "Since you cannot take *Amazing Grace* into Savannah, what is to become of me and my men?""

"You, the preacher, and your six crewmen will be released in one of your ship's boats. Like I told Pastor McClanahan, it's your decision whether to take those two rotting corpses with you, or to give them the watery burial they should have had long ago."

"And where will you take my ship?"

"Kings Town, Jamaica." Joshua pointed down to the main deck. "You have very little time to gather whatever you are taking with you, and to decide about the bodies."

"I'll tell my crew, and then I'll bring back Pastor McClanahan." As promised, the preacher and the captain were back with their decision. "We've decided that Matthew and Mark McTavish will be buried at sea."

"Then do it quickly so I can be underway."

As the preacher spoke the final words over the bodies, one of the *Amazing Grace* crewmen stepped next to Joshua and whispered. "I have a request, Captain Smoot."

"What is it?"

"My name is Tom Clark. I was born and raised in Jamaica. The Royal Navy impressed me and two others from our homes three years ago. I jumped ship and made my way to Falkirk where I worked at the docks until I was able to arrange working passage on *Amazing Grace*."

"So, you're trying to get back to Jamaica, and you want to join the prize crew to sail *Amazing Grace* there."

"Yes, if you would permit me to remain aboard."

"I don't see why not."

"Thank you, Captain Smoot."

☠ ☠ ☠

Two weeks later, the *Seacrest* and *Amazing Grace* arrived at the docks of Joshua's new friend, Charles Noble. As was their habit, nearly everybody within a mile of the waterfront was lining the docks as the two ships tied up. Charles and John Silver were the first up the gangway.

"Welcome to Kings Town, Captain Smoot. I was wondering when you'd bring me another prize."

"I've been busy at Savannah."

"That's what we've heard, Joshua." It was John Silver. "New docks, three cotton presses, a foundry, and a windmill that pumps water in and out of the rice fields, and mills both lumber and grist." He gave a laugh. "Too busy to keep the promise you made when you traded the *Seagull* for *Seacrest*?"

"I'll make it up to you, Mister Noble."

"I know you will, Joshua." He looked about the deck at the prize crew. "So, tell me about *Amazing Grace*. What's her cargo?"

Joshua pulled the shipping manifest from his pocket. "She sailed from Edinburgh, and except for the textiles and household items, most of her cargo is from the several iron works in the region."

"Hmm." Charles read down the list. "Printing presses and various weaving machines." He looked up. "Where were they taking these machines?"

"The captain told me they were taking some to Charles Town and the rest to New York City and Boston." Joshua gave a squint. "Are they worth something?"

"Only in the big northern cities, and only if you know the right people."

"And of course, you know those people?"

"Yes, I do."

"Aye, but first things first!" Silver pointed across the dock to his tavern. "My sweet wife Betty saw you coming before me, and put on a pot of your favorite lamb stew." He clapped his large hand onto Joshua's shoulder. "While you r crew gets ready for their well-deserved liberty, let's the three of us put down some ale, catch up on old times, and get full of the best cooking in Jamaica!"

"And while we're enjoying your hospitality, I'll have my shipwright do an inspection of *Amazing Grace* to see what she and her cargo are worth."

As was their habit, the pirates quickly descended on the various public houses for rum, landlubber's food, and female companionship—women of all ages, shapes, and sizes willing to trade their pretended virtue for the sailor's silver.

It was the next day when Charles Noble's shipwright came to him with the news. "Mister Noble!"

"What is it, Daniel?"

"You need to come with me to see something I found in *Amazing Grace*."

"What is it?"

"No—you need to see this for yourself."

"Very well." Charles put down his pencil and closed his journal. "Lead the way."

After climbing aboard the Scottish ship, Daniel descended the ladders to the bilges. He stopped and looked around to make certain they were alone.

"I heard about the two bodies, Daniel, and Captain Smoot assured me it was only cholera, not typhoid."

"It's not the disease, sir." He stepped down onto the stones and lifted several aside to expose the cannons. "It's these, sir." He spread his arms. "Except for a thin layer of stones, they used hundreds of Scottish carronades for ballast."

"Good Lord!" Charles looked across the stones. "There could be a thousand." He turned to the shipwright. "Does anybody else know about this—besides you and me?"

"No, sir. The moment I discovered them, I sent everybody from the ship."

"Put those stones back, have *Amazing Grace* moved down to the drydock, and once she's inside, close the doors." He looked across the ballast stones. "Captain Smoot told me that this ship was taking its cargo to Charles Town, New York City, and Boston."

"Then those cannons were meant for the revolution."

"Once the ship is secured, do not allow anybody back aboard until I return."

"Where are you going, sir?"

"I need to speak with my brother."

☠ ☠ ☠

John Silver was pouring ale and introducing whores to pirates when Charles Noble entered Silver Jack's Tavern. John looked up and called. "Charles! Over here! Come to join the party with these rich young sailors?"

"Uh…" He stepped to John and whispered. "We need to talk, privately."

"Oh?" Silver set down the pitcher and nodded toward the kitchen. Once the two were alone, John gave his adopted brother a tilt of his head. "What's going on?"

"Do you still want the treasure of Dead Man's Chest?"

It took John a moment. "What do you know, Charles?"

"First, tell me about my son's new friend."

"His name is John Paul Jones, but you already know that."

"Humor me, John, and tell me everything you know about him."

"Okay." The old pirate gave a disgusted huff. "Jones was a Scottish slaver who gave up the profession out of guilt to become a merchant captain. He killed a crewman at Tobago who was asking for his pay before he had earned it. Jones turned himself into the local magistrate, but he was told by a friend to flee Tobago because there were not enough British officers to hold a court martial, and the locals would have executed him. So, he fled from the island in the *Falmouth Packet*. He has been here in Kings Town for nearly a month."

"Do you know his intentions?"

"Your son, David, tells me that Jones wants to sail up to the colonies." He gave Charles a questioning look. "Is that enough?"

"Why does Jones want to go to the colonies?"

"David told me that Jones has a brother in Fredericksburg, and he has the deluded belief that he can talk his way into getting a naval commission."

"And why is it a delusion?"

"First, the continental naval commissions are only awarded to native-born men who have distinguished themselves as privateers." Silver held up two fingers. "Second, those distinguished privateer captains must present a letter of recommendation to the naval commission signed by the governor who issued their letter of marque."

"Anything else that disqualifies Jones?"

"Yes." John stepped to a small desk and opened the drawer. He held up a parchment. "This is the King's warrant for John Paul Jones' head."

"So, a deluded Scotsman with an outstanding King's warrant for his head, and none of the other requisite qualifications?"

Silver gave his younger brother a squint. "Why are we having this conversation, Charles?"

"Because I have discovered something that changes everything."

"Don't play games with me, Charles. What do you know that will help me—help both you and me —to get the rest of John Flint's treasure?"

"As you know, Joshua Smoot and I are in negotiations for the merchant-man *Amazing Grace*."

"Everybody in Kings Town knows that."

"There is something unique about *Amazing Grace* that I must tell you."

John Silver looked around the kitchen. "We're alone, so get to your point."

"My shipwright has finished his inspection of the prize ship. It is sound, and the cargo manifest is almost accurate."

"Almost?"

"He discovered something in the bilges."

"Go on."

"There are hundreds of new carronades hidden in her bilge as ballast—cannons that were being smuggled to the Americans."

"Really?" John Silver fell silent for several moments. "Besides you and your shipwright, who else knows about this?"

"Just you." Charles held up his hand. "Of course, the men Smoot set adrift near Savannah knew about the cannons, but they are long gone."

John Silver put a hand to his face and massaged his jaw while he thought. After several grunts and an equal number of sighs, the old pirate nodded. "I see it." John held up three fingers. "The cannons, the treasure, and that Scotsman's naval commission."

"My thoughts exactly, John."

"How long before you and Joshua must come to an agreement?"

"He's in no rush, so we can take our time."

"Good!" Silver pointed toward Charles' dock. "Go back and count the cannons while I think more about how I can leverage these things to our advantage."

That afternoon, Captain Smoot knocked on the door of Charles Noble's office.

"Come in, Joshua!" He poured two glasses of rum and pushed one across to the pirate.

"Have you come up with a price we can agree to?"

"*Amazing Grace* is sound, and the cargo is as the manifest says it is. There is no market for the machinery here in Jamaica, so I will have to pay a crew to sail her north where those machines can be sold. The rest will be stored and eventually sold to the locals, or used in trade to the coasters that frequent Kings Town."

"Of course." Joshua took a large sip of his rum. "Have you come up with a number?"

"Fifteen-thousand in silver, or—"

"Or what?"

"My shipwright is a curious man."

"Yes?"

"He took it upon himself to go aboard the *Seacrest*, and he told me that there are several parts of your ship that need repair—things that could cause catastrophic harm to the ship and your crew if not attended to."

"So, am I to understand that you want to repair my ship, and subtract the cost of those repairs from the fifteen-thousand?"

"No."

"Then what was your point in telling me that *Seacrest* needs work?"

"If you will follow me to our repair docks, I will show you."

Ten minutes later, the two stood looking out upon the three-masted French corvette with eleven cannons showing on her port side.

Joshua studied the beautiful ship for several breaths. "Who does that belong to?"

"It belongs to me."

"And why are you showing it to me?"

"Because I am willing to trade it for the two ships you sailed into Kings Town yesterday."

It took Joshua a moment to digest what Charles was offering. "Can I go aboard her?"

"Yes." Charles pointed down at a row boat. "We'll go together, Joshua."

Once on the deck, Joshua spread his arms. "I'll call her *Revenge*."

"She already has a perfect name."

"Oh?"

"Her name is *Le Tiburon*."

"The Shark."

"You know French?"

"No—only a few words."

"Well, her name is up to you."

"*Le Tiburon* will do." He gave Charles a smile. "So, tell me about her."

"She's 80 feet at the water line and 90 tons displacement. With her twenty-two guns, she's a match for the average British Navy's post ships."

"How did you come by her?"

"According to her log, she was built as a privateer in Teignmouth, Great Britain in '72 and transformed into a brig the following year at Torquay. She was heavily damaged in a storm and abandoned by her crew. I salvaged her and made the necessary repairs to bring her back as you now see her." He gave Joshua a nudge. "What do you think, Joshua? Your two ships for Le Tiburon?"

"I like her colors—red and black, with gold trim."

"Let's go below, starting at your cabin." A moment later, the two stepped into the spacious master's cabin. "Much nicer than your accommodations on *Seacrest*, wouldn't you say?"

"Why would you do this—trade me this perfect fighting ship for that merchantman and a ship needing repairs?"

"*Amazing Grace* is the first prize you've brought to me for the better part of a year. Perhaps with *Le Tiburon* at your command, your deliveries can become more frequent."

"Yes, they will."

"And that will more than compensate me for what you see as an uneven trade."

"Done!" Joshua took Charles' hand. "We have our agreement. You take *Amazing Grace*, her cargo, and *Seacrest*. I take *Le Tiburon*."

☠ ☠ ☠

When Charles reached his office, there was a young man standing with the shipwright.

"What's going on, Daniel? Who is this man, and what does he want?"

"He's…" Jack shook his head. "We had better step into your office, sir."

"Very well." Once inside, Charles turned on the stranger. "Who are you, and what do you want?"

"My name is Tom Clark. This morning, word reached Captain Smoot that there were hundreds of Scottish cannons hidden in *Amazing Grace's* bilge. He's coming tonight to take the cannons back."

"I remember you." Charles opened a drawer, pulled out a pistol, and set it on the desk between them. "You're one of his men—one of the prize crew that sailed *Amazing Grace* to my dock." Charles touched the pistol. "Why would one of Joshua Smoot's crewmen betray him to me?"

"I am a God-fearing man, sir. I don't want to see men killed needlessly over—"

"Stop!" Charles set down his glass, picked up the pistol and pulled back the lock. "The truth! Who are you?"

It took Joseph a long moment. He finally gave a sigh and a nod. "I'm not one of Smoot's men. I was part of the *Amazing Grace* crew, and when he was about to set the others adrift near Savannah, I volunteered to join the prize crew to bring her here to you."

"Why wouldn't you go with the others at Savannah?"

"I have family here in Jamaica, and I took working passage on *Amazing Grace* to eventually get here."

"Family, you say?" Charles set down the pistol. "Why would you need to lie about being one of Smoot's men when the truth was so simple?"

"I..."

"What about the cholera? Was that part of the scheme?"

"There was no cholera, sir, and nobody died."

"Then what was that nonsense Captain Smoot told us about two rotting bodies atop the ballast?"

"They were pig parts. It was part of the plan."

"I'll ask you again, and this time I expect an honest answer. Who are you, and what is your connection to those cannons?"

It took him a long moment. "My name is Joseph Reed. I was born and raised in New Jersey. I am a graduate of the College of New Jersey. I am a member of Philadelphia's Committee of Correspondence. I am an aide-de-camp to General George Washington."

"Go on."

"I was sent to Falkirk, Scotland to purchase the carronades that the Royal Navy had rejected. I was to deliver them to the general at Fredericksburg."

"And now that I own them, what do you intend to do?"

"Since a war is coming, the cannons must eventually get to General Washington for the defense of America. I am authorized by the Continental Army to negotiate with you for their return."

"I'm not open to negotiations at this time, so I suggest you go back and continue to play your part as Tom Clark."

"I'm serious, sir. Smoot and his men are coming after dark to take those cannons from you."

"We'll see about that."

☠ ☠ ☠

Charles appointed his son David as lookout. Just after six, the thirteen angry men marched west along the docks from *Le Tiburon* toward the Noble warehouse.

"Father!" David gave an apologetic nod to several of the guests and pointed. "They're coming."

"How many?"

"It looks like a dozen or so, and Smoot is leading them."

"You'll have to excuse me, Colonel Lewis. I need to step outside to welcome several more arriving guests."

"More women?"

"I'll go see." Charles followed David to the warehouse door and the two walked out onto the dock.

"There they are, Father." He counted quickly. "Captain Smoot and a dozen of his men."

The pirates stopped twenty feet short of the two with drawn weapons. "You knew I would come!"

"Ah!" Charles pointed back at the warehouse. "Come to join the party, have you?"

"No! I'm here to get my cannons!"

"Your cannons?" He gave a laugh. "By what authority?"

"They were hidden under the ballast. I didn't know they were there until this morning."

"Neither did I, and we both negotiated our agreement upon that same ignorance."

Smoot pointed his pistol at the merchant. "Choose, Mister Noble. You can give me the cannons and live, or I will take them over your dead body."

Just then, three British officers and their ladies pushed out through the door with drinks in hand. "Charles! What's taking so long, and who are those men?"

"These are men from *Le Tiburon*, that French corvette being outfitted at the other end of my dock. They heard I was hosting a party for the King's birthday, and wondered if they could join us."

"Uh, they look a rough bunch, Charles." One of the women leaned close and whispered to the colonel. He gave a nod and turned back to the pirates. "I don't believe our ladies would welcome the presence of men like you." The woman gave him a nudge. "Oh, and she said you don't smell very nice either."

"You heard him, Captain Smoot." Charles stepped close to the pirate and lowered his voice. "There are fifty armed British soldiers from Fort Augusta in the warehouse. Are you certain you want to press me for the cannons right now?"

"Damn you, Charles Noble!" He put away his pistol and backed away. "Damn you to hell!"

When John Silver reached the warehouse, Charles was waiting with two glasses of rum. "Okay, big brother. Why this meeting? Have you changed the plan we agreed to already?"

"No changes—just some assurance that we're in full agreement about your son." Silver took the drink and pulled a list from his pocket. "The young Scotsman's ship—the *Falmouth Packet*—is now fitted with those four small cannons and a standard supply of powder and shot. The provisions for the trip are being loaded as we speak, and I've found four men who want to sign on for working passage to Virginia."

"Yes—as we planned." Charles took the list and set it on the desk. "But your tone of voice suggests that something is bothering you."

"It's David." Silver refilled his drink. "Are you certain he understands his mission—that he is to guide Captain Jones toward my three-part plan—that Jones can earn a naval commission by bringing us the treasure of Dead Man's Chest to buy the cannons from you for the Americans?"

"David understands his part, John. We've had several long talks, and he is a trustworthy lad. He will do as I've told him."

"And you're certain Captain Jones saw the cannons?"

"Oh, yes." Charles gave a nod. "He was very aware of them."

"One other thing."

"Yes?"

"It's essential that the *Falmouth Packet* leaves before dawn so that Joshua Smoot does not know of their departure."

"You truly fear that Smoot would take David hostage to get my cannons?"

"Joshua Smoot has a blacker soul than me, and if I was in his place, I would not hesitate to kidnap your son for those cannons."

Early the next morning, just as the sun was pinking the sky, David Noble, John Paul Jones, and their crew of four set sail from Kings Town for Fredericksburg. The swift little craft rounded the ruins of Port Royal as the pirates rose for another day of outfitting their new ship.

The mid-watch knocked at Joshua's cabin door. Captain smoot looked up from his papers. "Not now!"

"Captain Smoot!"

"I said, not now!"

"I know, Captain, but you're going to want to hear this!"

"Then come in and tell me what you think I want to hear!"

"You told me to watch the Noble warehouse and the cannons."

Joshua looked up from his papers. "Has something changed? Has he done something with the cannons?"

"No, Captain, they're still in his main warehouse."

"Then what is so pressing that you felt that you needed to interrupt me?"

"It's David Noble."

"Damn!" Joshua struck the table with his fist. "We were not to kidnap him until *Le Tiburon* was ready to sail!"

"We haven't kidnapped him yet, Captain."

"Then what is it about the lad that I must know?"

"The *Falmouth Packet* set sail before sunrise."

"And why would you think that should concern me?"

"David Noble was aboard."

"Damn!" Joshua pushed the papers aside and stared at the man. "Call the men who are overseeing the fitting of *Le Tiburon*."

"Sir?"

"I need to know how soon we can get underway."

"Aye, aye, Captain."

CHAPTER TWENTY-ONE:
Damaged Rudder

*I*t took the *Falmouth Packet* a day to reach the Windward Passage. Once clear, John Paul Jones altered course to take advantage of the gulf stream to skirt the northern coast of Cuba, and then turned starboard toward the southern tip of Florida. Four days later, as the swift little craft raced along the Georgia coast, *Le Tiburon* finally caught up and spotted the fleeing craft.

"Is it them, Cap'n?" It was Danny Turner, one of the men Jack Bridger had recommended to Joshua. "Is it the *Falmouth Packet*?"

"Aye." Joshua lowered the glass and turned to the new bosun. "It's not clear how many others are aboard, but no matter what it takes to capture them, nobody is to be killed until I have David Noble safe and sound aboard *Le Tiburon*. Is that clear?"

"Aye, but word is that they may have a cannon or two aboard. What if they fire on us, Captain?"

"We will deal with that as we must."

"I understand."

Le Tiburon overtook the *Falmouth Packet* ten miles south of the Savannah River. Following Captain Smoot's orders, all twenty cannons were loaded and primed, and six of the crew stood by with grappling hooks.

"On deck!" Joshua shouted to the men as *Le Tiburon* passed abeam the *Falmouth Packet*. "Spill the sails and stand by with grappling hooks!" He turned to the helmsman. "When I tell you, turn into them so our gunwales collide!"

"Aye, Captain!"

"Do you think they might be carrying any booty?"

"It isn't booty I want, Danny."

"I know you want David Noble for ransom, Cap'n, but they might still be carrying something of value that the crew can split up."

Smoot turned to his young first mate. "Once I have David Noble, I don't care what you and the others do with that ship or the rest of her crew."

Danny smiled and looked again at the fleeing packet a half league ahead. "Look at her, Cap'n! Why, she'll be easier to take than a maiden's favors in springtime. Ha! Ha!" He stepped to the rail and pointed with his cutlass. "She's just asking to be plucked like the sweet fruit she is!"

"She looks harmless enough, but don't underestimate her, Danny. One or two well-aimed balls from one of her cannons could take down one of our masts or set us afire." He handed the glass back to Daniel. "Here."

He studied their prey. "All I see are two swivel guns—one on her bow and the other on her poop. If she has any cannons, then they're not run out yet." He lowered the glass. "Them postal packets got sails, not cannons."

"Just the same, Danny, watch yourself. Over confidence accounts for there being not many old pirates alive to brag about their bravery."

Daniel looked up at their flag. "Can I run up the red flag, Cap'n?"

"Yes. It's time we signal our intentions."

A moment later, the no quarter flag replaced the skull and crossed cutlasses, and was met by the demonic cheers of the crew.

☠ ☠ ☠

Captain Jones called to his crew. "We've precious little time before she's within range, so let's step lively. I'll man the helm while you five make ready for battle."

The men scattered themselves about the deck in what appeared at first to be mass confusion. Several sheets to lee were released, and their counterparts to weather were hauled. From the midst of the confusion emerged a well-planned and executed set of tasks that had the little ship set wing-and-wing for the run downwind.

Seamus ran aft and knuckled his forelock. "A word, Cap'n Jones?"

"Make it quick!"

"Those other three are scared. None of them have ever seen a real battle at sea, only the stories."

"We're all scared, Seamus!"

"They want to know if we have to fight. They want to know if we'd stand a better chance if we struck our colors and raised a white flag."

Captain Jones pointed at *Le Tiburon*. "You, more than any of us, should know what that red flag means!"

"It means no quarter, Cap'n. I've seen it before."

"They intend to kill us for our cargo. Wouldn't you rather die standing and fighting rather than on your knees?"

"Well…"

"I don't have time for this! Tell the others I have a plan—that we have a good chance of coming through this alive!"

"But we don't, Cap'n!" The Irishman looked aft at the approaching ship. "We're outnumbered twenty to one!"

"A crew without hope is dead already!" John pointed forward. "I want all the small arms loaded and stacked at the rails, with plenty of ammunition. We'll also need two axes at each rail to cut grappling hooks." The man hesitated. "Now!"

While the Irishman ran forward, John called to the young Italian. "Carini! As soon as you've secured those lines, break out the medical supplies and put all the irons we have on the fire. If we survive this, there's sure to be casualties."

"The irons?"

"You've cauterized a wound before, haven't you, Mario?"

Carini trotted aft and stopped several yards away from John. "No sir, not me."

"Oh, Lord!" John glanced back at the pirate ship. "I'm probably the only one who's been in battle!"

After some hasty instructions, the Italian ran forward, dropped below deck, and set to his task.

While the *Falmouth Packet* fled toward the safety of shore five leagues to the west, *Le Tiburon* closed quickly for her first kill.

"What do you think, sir?" David pointed to an inlet among the string of small islands. "Can we make that inlet with this canvas, or would we stand a better chance by reaching for that other one further north?"

"Our only hope is on a direct run, wing and wing. On that course, I'm hoping *Le Tiburon*'s aft sails will block her fore sails and perhaps give us the edge we need." John laid a hip to the tiller and looked aft once more at their pursuer. The enemy ship was now less than a thousand yards away.

"Damn!" John looked to the men at work at the cannons. "Barragan, Etinger! Are your cannons loaded and ready?"

"Aye, Cap'n!" Seamus stood out of respect while he answered. "Both fore guns be loaded with grape shot an' the aft two be carryin' bar stock, just as you ordered."

No sooner had Barragan joined the others at the larboard cannons than *Le Tiburon* made a course change. Like every student of blue water warfare, John recognized the tactic.

"Once she's in position, she'll spill her sails and back down just enough so our gunwales meet! That's when they'll throw their grappling hooks!"

Le Tiburon was now nearly parallel to the little packet and closing quickly. Suddenly, there was an explosion from one of the larger ship's guns, followed by a sickening shudder along the entire length of the smaller ship's frame.

"How could they be so stupid?" John let go the tiller just long enough to look over the starboard rail. Two jagged rows of splinters raised pivot-like on the ship's ribs where the ball had pierced the oak planking below the waterline—one of the worst hits a ship could take. He grabbed the tiller just as *Le Tiburon* luffed her first sheet for her backing-down maneuver.

"Ready on both starboard cannons!" John watched for the exact moment. "Stand by! Sand by! Fire!"

Both starboard cannons kicked aft as their deadly loads ripped at *Le Tiburon*'s great stern. The bar stock took a large chunk off the upper edge of the rudder while the second cannon's grapeshot peppered the master's cabin, breaking out most of the larboard windows.

John threw the tiller hard to larboard and called. "Barragan, Clark, stand ready at your cannons!"

Both seamen crouched next to their pieces, linstocks held just above the touchholes. By now, the *Falmouth Packet* was well into its starboard turn behind *Le Tiburon*'s stern, avoiding the rest of the larger vessel's broadside. They all watched with gritted teeth while the Falmouth's bowsprit clipped the great lantern hanging from the larger ship's taffrail, sending it twisting as it fell end-over-end into the dark blue water.

Startled at this unexpected change in their plans, Smoot and Danny ran aft and peered down at the little ship passing under their stern. Captain Jones's eyes met Smoot's for several angry seconds.

"Ready now…fire!"

Seamus's linstock dropped an inch and ignited the powder in the cannon's base ring. The primer flashed brightly, followed an instant later by the twelve-pounder belching forth its deadly load of grapeshot at the great ship. The crew of the *Falmouth Packet* would never know how effective that third shot had been, for it stopped *Le Tiburon*'s attack completely. Inside the cloud of white smoke, the spreading pellets ripped upward through the larger ship's taffrail and into her lower rigging. Daniel Turner and six feet of polished rail were now raining over *Le Tiburon*'s foredeck and sails in a grisly shower of mahogany splinters, blood, shattered bones, and various other body parts.

Not having the time or the manpower to trim the sails for their starboard reach, the *Falmouth Packet* lost much, if not all her headway. Before the acrid cloud of their first larboard shot had cleared, *Le Tiburon*'s great rudder began to pass the second cannon.

It only took a whisper from Captain Jones. "Fire!" The second cannon barked forth its destructive bar stock.

For several moments, the smoke from both cannons hung between the two ships, obscuring not only the setting sun, but the entire stern of the ominous foe that towered over the small postal ship. Then, as if a blacksmith's hut had been caught up in a tornado, oak and mahogany splinters, enormous pieces of flat iron and bolts, began to rain down onto the smaller ship's deck. Whatever the iron projectile had hit, it was working.

Le Tiburon lost all headway and began a slow turn to larboard.

"Larboard cannons, reload with bar stock! Starboard crew, haul in the starboard sheets and trim for a larboard reach!" Captain Jones turned and shouted at David. "Take the helm, and as soon as we're at a hundred yards, come about to a starboard beam reach! We've a hole below the starboard water line aft, and we'll sink if we don't keep her heeled over!"

John and the four seamen set about their tasks while David watched the wind to select the optimum course. As ordered, he turned back to the heading they had followed before *Le Tiburon's* attack.

"That's good!" John called aft, looking to *Le Tiburon* again. She was still floundering. "Hold that heading until we can assess damage and get a wet patch on that hole!"

David pushed the tiller back to midships and then looked about at the pirates. "Look, Captain!" He pointed. "Her rudder! The upper half is gone! We beat her!"

"Aye, we beat her, but we've no time to glory in our victory until we can get out of range and patch that hole."

Their cannons now reloaded, Seamus and Clark joined the others hauling the mainsail sheet to bring the great boom directly over the helm.

Once the ship was trimmed on the new course, John stepped to the Irishman. "Barragan, you claimed you've some carpentry experience. Is that true?"

"Aye, Cap'n! I were a planker an' caulker at—"

John didn't want to listen to the man's lengthy story. "Can you make up a canvas patch?" Before Seamus could answer, a ball from one of the pirate's forward swivel guns whistled overhead. Everyone ducked, as the ball punched through the mainsail.

"I never done it 'afore, Cap'n, but I've seen it once on that man-o'-war I were tellin' ya 'bout. Cap'n Jenkins told me he'd—"

"Do your best, Barragan." John descended the short ladder that led to his cabin. The deck was flooded, but the hole was now high enough above the sea that the flood had stopped. He immediately saw what had prevented the ball from continuing through and out the other side of the ship. In the center of the deck, where it had been pushed by the impact, lay the anchor chain. Setting within its rusted links was the single six-inch ball. While John returned to the main deck, another one of the pirate's swivel guns fired, punching a hole in the flying jib.

At a thousand yards from the floundering pirate ship and well beyond their swivel guns, David turned the *Falmouth Packet* into the wind just long enough for the crew to grab the mainsail boom and pull it over the deck, flat against the wind, bringing the small ship to a crawl.

Adjusting the jib and mainsail held the wind on the starboard beam, keeping the little ship heeled over far enough to lift the hole well above the water until the canvas patch was in place. Clark and Etinger—being the better swimmers—volunteered to pull the two larboard ropes under the keel to hold the lower two corners in place. Within an hour, the *Falmouth Packet* was once again underway but no longer headed for Virginia.

"David, once we're underway, set a course for the Savannah River. That's where we'll make our repairs."

"No!" David shook his head. "We can't go to Savannah."

"Why not?"

"Because that's where Smoot will take *Le Tiburon*."

"Oh?"

"He has a home on the bluff east of the town and he's in league with most of the Savannah merchants."

John walked to the hatch and called. "Barragan!"

"Sir?"

"Will that patch hold for three days?"

Seamus looked aft at the man on the pump and called back. "I heard what Master Noble told you about Smoot and Savannah! We have no choice but to make it to Charles Town, Cap'n."

John turned back to David. "This will be better. I know the owner of a shipyard in Charles Town."

That afternoon, Captain Jones and his crew sailed past the newly-built Morris Island Lighthouse and into Charles Town harbor. The water was teeming with departing and returning coasters and merchant ships of every size and description. The *Falmouth Packet* sailed to the southern end of East Bay Street and twenty yards from the end of Broad Street. With less than two hours of sunlight remaining, John and David rowed ashore to arrange for repairs

Seamus called to them upon their return. "What did they say, Cap'n? Is there a place where we can careen her?"

"Tipton's Dock." John pointing up the Cooper River. "They have a stretch of open beach we can use. Can you and the others manage to get her on the beach and get her hauled down for repairs without David and me?"

"Aye Cap'n." Seamus gave a nervous look back at the three others. "Will you and Master Noble be stayin' ashore for the night?"

John nodded while the small boat bumped against the Falmouth's hull. "I have to sign in at the Harbor Master's office and deliver the mail, and then we have some other business to conduct." John fished through the inside pocket of his waistcoat and produced a handful of silver coins. "Don't wait for us. Here's enough money to purchase the wood you'll need to patch those three planks, and some extra for you and your mates to get dinner and drinks. Get as much done tonight as you can, and then take your mates into town."

Seamus took the coins and knuckled his forelock. "Aye, aye, Cap'n!"

John pushed away and David began pulling on the sweeps.

Seamus called after them. "You and Master Noble watch yourselves, now! I been here 'afore an' there be some rough characters in some o' them taverns!"

John held up his sword and David opened his waistcoat to reveal the two fowling pistols. "Don't worry! We can take care of ourselves."

Like Kings Town, Charles Town had its long row of taverns strewn along the docks, catering to the needs of the men who had just come up from the sea. It was neither by tradition, nor design that these public houses served as the collection points for word from the four points of the compass.

John and David headed for the Patriot's Rest Tavern. Once inside, they chose a small table at the back of the public room, near several well-dressed businessmen. The oldest of the four was very angry, so it wasn't difficult to overhear his conversation. John and David took their seats, catching the older man in mid-sentence.

"...taken about all they can, James. If the damned parliament does not back off soon, they're going to be up to here in—" He broke off when the younger man on his left put a hand of caution to his arm. With a quick look about the tavern for strangers and loyalists, the older man leaned forward and continued in a quieter voice. "Word's come from the Committees of Correspondence in Virginia of some trouble in Boston Harbor in protest of this bloody tea tax. I read the letter myself and recognized the signatures of both Patrick Henry and Thomas Jefferson. Seems some Indians boarded the merchantman *Beaver* and dumped the entire shipment of monopoly brick tea into the harbor. And there's a rumor that the Indian chief's name was Sam Adams." The other three roared with laughter.

"Then that explains why the local customs officers locked up the East India Company warehouses the other day." It was a younger man in a beaver hat.

"They must be afraid that a group of Charles Town Indians will dump their tea in the harbor too."

The older man raised his hand. "The crown will, of course, retaliate. I have just heard from London that the port of Boston is now closed. No ships will go in or out until the tea is paid for." Shock and surprise ran through the room. "And it is now illegal to have any sort of public meeting in Boston." This provoked cries of outrage and disbelief. "There's more, gentlemen. The same letter told of a new Quartering Act, which will apply, not just to Massachusetts but to all the colonies."

"That's not news, sir." It was the man in black. "They're already allowing soldiers to take quarters in taverns and unoccupied buildings."

"You don't understand James. The new law expands that to include private homes." He looked at each man in turn. "This is most serious."

The others waited.

"Not only will the home owners have to take the food from their own mouths to feed the lobster backs, but they'll be forced to put their children on the floor so the soldiers have a comfortable bed."

The man in the beaver hat slapped the table, causing most of the clientele to look at the five men. "I'll be damned before any soldier's going to move into *my* house and eat *my* food!" The others tried to calm him. "Mother England's sitting on her brain again, and this time she's going to get bit!"

"You can thank Lord North for that. These new laws are his doing, and he's pushing us right into war."

"You don't know how prophetic your last words are, Christopher." It was the older gentleman speaking, once again just above a whisper. "There's strong evidence that most of the members of the Marine Committee have been chosen, and that Esek Hopkins will be selected as Commander in Chief of the Continental Navy."

One of the others reached across and put a hand on the forearm of the white-haired man who had not spoken yet. "But why not you, Mister Forrestal?

"I've the name but not the military background for it, William. No, Hopkins would be the best choice. Besides, I'm too old and broken in body for the strain."

"How soon do you think they'll be outfitting ships and selecting the men to man them?"

Forrestal leaned forward. "I laid the keels for two large Dutch brigs at my yard several months ago, William, and I expect them to be ready to float within six months. Depending on the decisions made between now and then, they can become merchantmen or armed frigates."

The younger of the five men stood, raised his tankard and his voice. "Gentlemen! A toast!" Everybody in the tavern stood. "To freedom!" Everyone drank, then retook their seats. The younger man continued. "Surely God is on the side of freedom." From all around the tavern came echoing shouts of agreement.

John and David had heard enough. A Continental Navy was more than just a rumor. They downed their drinks and left the tavern to look for the provisions they would need to continue their trip to Fredericksburg.

CHAPTER TWENTY-TWO:
Windmill and Leverage

*T*he winds blew steady from the southeast, allowing *Le Tiburon* to sail the fifteen miles from the Atlantic Ocean to the new saw mill dock to the east of Lamar's Creek. As the hawsers were thrown across, Willem Kesteren, Isaac, and Aaron Attucks made a quick inspection of the damage to the rear of *Le Tiburon*.

"Welcome home, Captain Smoot!" While Joshua walked down to the dock, Willem approached and held out a hand of greeting. "It's been over a month since you left, and from the looks of things, you've quite a story to tell."

"Captain Smoot!" It was Isaac Attucks. He and Aaron stood at *Le Tiburon's* stern studying the web of lines that now controlled the remains of the shattered rudder. "It's a fine ship you've brought here, but what happened to your rudder?"

"Obviously, Isaac, we came up against a foe that got in a lucky shot."

"Was it one of the Brits at the blockade?"

"Make a hole!" Four of the crewmen marched down the gangway with their bags. One of them stopped and spit at Joshua's feet. "That wasn't a mutiny, Captain Smoot! Those two men you killed only asked for a foc'sal counsel to ask—"

"You weren't there, Jenkins. You didn't hear when he and those others threatened me with a mutiny."

"So, you're telling us that they lied to us—that you didn't tell Pritchard to turn when he did?"

"They told you what you wanted to hear." He pointed up at the ship. "He followed my orders and turned when he was supposed to." While they spoke, several dozen more disgruntled crewmen walked down to the dock and assembled behind Jenkins.

"Listen up!" Joshua stepped up onto a stack of fresh cut lumber. "None of you signed on with the promise that we would take a prize, so you go away as you came—empty-handed."

"You told us that the *Falmouth Packet* would be carrying a cargo worth the attack."

"I told you that..." Joshua looked at Willem and back to the seven. "You know as well as I do that every ship has something worth taking, and you also know that postal packets are never armed."

"Well, that one was, and now three men are dead because you insisted that we attack her." The man raised a hand and made a filthy gesture. "A curse on you, Pritchard, and *Le Tiburon*!"

"Uh..." Willem waited until the men were gone. "I was going to give you a tour of the factories, but that can wait, Joshua."

"I'm sorry." Joshua gave a frustrated huff. "Nothing went as I hoped, and..."

"So, would you rather that I give you a while to get yourself together?"

"I'm together. I'm just angry at myself for several bad decisions." Joshua took a large breath and looked around at the log decks and stacks of hewn lumber. "You've done a lot of work in these six weeks, Willem."

"Yes, and I've hired your sister to oversee everything in your absence."

"Sarah works for me?"

"Yes, and she moved the business ledgers into High Tortuga. I hope you don't mind her setting up her office in the library."

"Not at all. It can get quite lonely being in that large house by myself." Joshua turned to the Attucks brothers. "I assume you two have settled into running the windmill and its various operations."

"Oh, yes." Aaron pointed to the stacks of lumber. "I'm running the sawmill and Isaac is running the gristmill."

Willem stepped between the two. "They are in daily arguments over which operation is to run first."

"Alright." Joshua looked across the creek at the western docks and the string of buildings. "Lead the way, Willem. Show me everything you've done."

"Of course." Willem gave the brothers a nod and ushered Joshua to a new dam across the creek. "Look down in the water, Joshua. Those are the Archimedes Screws that move the water in and out of the canal." He pointed to the windmill. "There's an underground shaft that contains the drive mechanism." He pointed to the west docks and warehouses. "Come."

"I've expanded the dock to two-hundred yards, which has allowed the building of two large warehouses." He pointer. "As you can see, we've added several buildings that weren't here when you left."

"Uh...?" Joshua stopped and looked at the signs over the doors. "Savannah Tyler Press? A. N. Miller Press? Lamar's Hydraulic Cotton Press? Miller's Foundry?" He looked back at the windmill. "Anderson's Wharf and Robert's Street Saw and

Grist Mill?" He looked at Willem. "You'll have to explain the name thing to me. Why aren't they named after me?"

"You own everything—the docks, the windmill, these buildings, and everything that goes on inside them."

"Then why aren't they named after me?"

"Because the people we serve want to deal with the merchants of Savannah—the names on the signs—not a notorious pirate."

"Ah, I see." Joshua turned and pointed at the two-story brick building to the south. "What goes on in that building?"

"With the trees that come to the sawmill, there is an abundance of pine sap. You are producing turpentine and rosin—the ingredients for making varnish and several other products used to repair ships." Willem pointed back at Le Tiburon. "Why don't you go up to High Tortuga and get some rest. I'll come up later and tell you what it will take to repair your ship."

"Yes, and it will give me a chance to confer with my sister."

☠ ☠ ☠

The next year passed slowly for Joshua. Le Tiburon was repaired and sent to sea on a regular schedule under the command of Nate Prichard—the coxswain who stood with Joshua when most of the crew left. He had taken up a pipe and reading novels to pass the time.

He put his marker at the page, closed the book, and looked across at her. "Sarah, can we talk for a moment?"

"Of course." She looked up from her ledger and set down her quill. "More tea?"

"No, I…"

"What's the matter, Joshua? You haven't been yourself for some time now."

"I'm still worried that Robert Ormerod is hunting for me for what happened to his daughter."

"I thought that you had gotten over that—that he's searching for John Manley of Jamaica, not Joshua Smoot of Savannah."

"I know, but if he is anything like me, he will never give up."

"How long has it been?"

"Nearly a year."

"Oh, my little brother." She gave a huff and turned in her chair. "You have to get over this and look at how God has blessed you." He looked at her but did not answer. "Everything is as it should be." She pointed east. "The windmill is running at capacity." She put a hand on the journal. "The rice farmers are prospering and paying their monthly fees on time. Our warehouses are full, and when the merchants ask that we take one of the inbound ships, Pritchard and the prize crew can be counted on." She gave Joshua a smile. "This is exactly what you wanted."

"I understand what you're saying, Sarah. I know I should be satisfied with all that I have but something…"

"It's the chase. It's the capture." Sarah looked at the clock and checked her notes. "Does the meeting you had me arrange with Mister Lamar today have something to do with this?"

"Yes. Governor Wright borrowed a great sum of money from the merchants of Savannah last year, and his debt came due this month. He was unable to pay and asked that he be given more time to raise the money."

"Yes, I remember hearing about that." She gave him a questioning look. "If I may ask, what does that have to do with you?"

"Leverage." Joshua gave a nod and continued. "I am going to ask Basil Lamar to send the governor a letter offering to forgive his debt if he will come to Savannah to meet with me."

"Are we signing some sort of contract with the governor?"

"No. I want Governor Wright to grant me a letter of marque so that I can continue doing what I do but without the constant threat of the gallows."

"And if the governor refuses to give you this letter, will that affect the mill or any of the other factories at Lamar's Creek?"

"No." Joshua stood. "Everything will continue as it is."

"Good." She looked at the clock. "The cook will have dinner ready at five. Will you be back by then?"

"Yes." With a quick stop at his study to retrieve a packet of money, Joshua stepped from the porch and climbed into his carriage. "Take me to the Lamar Cotton Exchange."

Basil Lamar was waiting and invited him into his office. "So, what is this pressing matter you wanted to discuss with me, Joshua?"

"Am I correct that Governor Wright is still in debt to you?"

"I…" Basil pinched his lower lip between his thumb and finger. "You know very well that I have made it my policy to not discuss the financial circumstances of one client with another client."

"Yes, and I appreciate that." Joshua set his satchel on the desk, pulled out the packet, and untied the string. "According to my agent, Governor Wright borrowed twenty-thousand pounds from you several years ago to fund his campaign, and to build his Atlanta mansion." He pushed the money across the desk. "I am willing to pay his debt in exchange for your help with a personal matter."

"You want Governor Wright to come to Savannah to issue you a letter of marque."

"You know about that?"

"I know most everything that goes on in Savannah, and like you, I have eyes and ears working for me in Atlanta."

"Be that as it may, I'm asking you to summon Governor Wright to Savannah to meet with me."

"Do you want him to know that it is you who is paying his debt?"

"No" Joshua considered. "Feel free to make up anything you want about yours and my relationship as long as it gets him to come to High Tortuga—my mansion—to meet and talk with me."

"You do know that Governor James Wright is the last British Royal Governor in the colonies."

"Yes—I know that."

"And you are aware that he is holding a personal grudge against you for taking a ship in which he had invested heavily."

"I just need a face-to-face with him at my home to request that letter of marque."

"Very well." Basil took the money and put it in his safe. "Naturally, if he refuses to come to Savannah, I will return your money."

"Naturally."

Basil locked the safe, turned, and offered his hand. "I will send a letter to him and let you know his answer as soon as I hear from him."

"Thank you."

Two weeks passed without word, and then Basil Lamar knocked on Joshua's door.

"Basil! Come in and tell me what you have heard from the governor."

"He's agreed to see you."

"Very well." Joshua gave a smile. "Once he and I have that meeting, his debt is paid in full."

"He's due tomorrow at noon."

☠ ☠ ☠

The next day, a carriage rolled to a stop in front of Joshua's mansion at three minutes before noon. Sarah stood in the foyer and looked out through the rain. She turned and looked at the clock. "Governor Wright isn't your friend, Joshua, but he's certainly a punctual man."

"Aye." He walked across the foyer to her side and looked through the window as the man stepped down and pulled his coat up against the rain. "We're going to need some privacy. I hope you do not mind."

"Not at all." She looked toward the hallway. "I think I'll go down to the kitchen and ask Molly to make me a sandwich." She hesitated at the door. "Do you want her to bring something up for you and the governor?"

"No, but thank you for asking." Joshua stepped out onto the porch and extended a hand to the older man. "Welcome to High Tortuga, Governor Wright."

Ignoring Joshua's hand, the governor pushed past with a huff.

"You must be cold, Governor." Joshua followed into the foyer and pointed across to the study. "There's a brisk fire burning in my study, along with cigars and my best Jamaican rum."

"No!" The governor turned and pointed an accusing finger at the pirate. "I'm here under protest. Your pretended kindness is wasted on me."

"Really? After all that I've done for you and the colony of Georgia."

"I'll admit that, like your father before you, your piracies have helped Savannah in many ways. But as the King's appointed governor of Georgia, I cannot betray my oath of office by getting in league with a pirate."

"I wish you would look at this from another perspective." Joshua walked to his desk and picked up a stack of money. "We all have debts that must be paid. We all have people with needs.

"The only reason I am here is because Basil Lamar made this visit the price for forgive my debt to him."

"A wonderful gesture by Basil indeed." Joshua held up the money. "This is ten-thousand dollars. It would pay for your daughter's education at Oxford or one of the other universities in England."

"Keep your blood money, Smoot. I know you want to buy a letter of marque, but you'll never see my signature on any document that contains your name, except to order your execution." With that, the governor stepped to the door and put on his hat.

"Where are you going?"

"Back to Atlanta." The governor pulled open the front door allowing the rain and leaves to blow into the foyer. "My business here is finished, and you can count yourself fortunate that I even came. Now that I've fulfilled my promise to Lamar, I hope to never see your evil face again, except with the hangman's noose pulled tight against the side of your head—right next to that scar you richly deserved."

"I'll get that letter of marque, one way or another, Governor Wright. You can lay odds to that."

"One way or another?" He stopped and turned in the open doorway. "You aren't so presumptuous or so stupid as to think you can threaten the King's governor of Georgia, are you?"

"Oh, it's much more than a threat." He held up the money. "And I'll get me letter of marque someday without paying a bribe."

"And you, Joshua Smoot, can expect a visit from the local constable for that promise!"

"Ha!" Joshua raised a fist. "Constable Gilmore is one of my closest friends and wealthiest accomplices in Savannah." With a laugh, Joshua slammed the door behind the man and returned to his study.

Halfway down the walk toward his waiting carriage, the governor stopped and looked to a young man standing next to a live oak. "I suppose you're one of his crewmen hoping I'd help you cheat the gallows too."

"The gallows?" Henry looked to the mansion and back to the governor. "Who are you?"

"I'm James Wright—the King's Governor of Georgia—the man who will arrest and hang Joshua Smoot for piracy." With that, the governor climbed into his carriage.

"Damn!" Henry pulled a piece of white cloth from his shirt, stepped back to the tree, and called out toward the mansion. "Captain Smoot!"

"Ha!" Joshua picked up the bundle of cash. "So, you've changed your mind and want this bribe after all." Joshua walked across the foyer and pulled the door open just in time to see the carriage turn around and drive away.

"Who called my name?" Joshua pulled the pistol from his belt. "If you've come from New York to take revenge for—"

"Belay!" Henry held out the cloth and waved it up and down. "It's me, Captain!"

"Step away from that tree and show yourself!" Joshua stepped to the edge of the porch and leveled his pistol at the tree.

"A parley, Captain Smoot!" Henry gave the cloth another wave.

"Whoever you are, be advised that I am in a bad mood!" He pulled back the hammer on his pistol. "Show yourself now, or by John Flint's black heart, I'll march over there and kill you where you stand!"

"Belay, Captain!" Henry peeked around the edge of the tree. "Don't shoot me 'till you've heard what I came to tell you!"

"Morgan?" He lowered the pistol. "Is that you, Henry Morgan?"

"Aye, in the flesh!" The young man took a half step from cover but kept a hand on the tree. "I've got something important that you're gonna want to hear!"

"How dare you come here while Robert Ormerod is hunting me?"

"Nobody followed me, Captain. I made sure of that!"

"We killed his little girl. He'll never stop looking for us!"

"I know, but you gotta let me say my piece before you send me away!"

"Make it quick and then be gone!"

Henry took another step from the tree. "Do you remember our talk on the way to New York—what you told me about John Silver's map?"

"What about it?"

"You told me that there was something else going on—that neither Charles Noble nor Long John Silver would hand us *Seacrest* and all those provisions for some sentimental keepsake on some island in the Antilles!"

"I remember! What about it?"

"Well, you were right! There was a lot more to it!"

"Walk up here so we can quit yelling through the rain!"

"I'll tell you, but first I need to know if you're still out to kill me for letting Jane Ormerod burn up in that fire!"

"I could lie to you and tell you that time has healed that wound, but it would be easier for me to march out there and shoot you where you stand!"

"No!" Henry retreated to the protection of the tree. "I need a ten-minute truce for what I came to tell you, and another ten minutes to negotiate my share!"

"Your share of what?"

"The truce! Do you grant it to me or not?"

"You chose a dark day for this, Henry, so don't play one of your guessing games with me!"

"You're gonna want to hear what I have to tell you, Captain! But I gotta know you're not going to shoot me when I show myself!"

"Alright!" Joshua pushed the pistol into his belt and held his arms to the side. "A truce!"

"You swear that on John Flint's black heart?"

"Yes!"

"Say it, Captain!" Henry put a hand to his ear. "I need to hear you say the words."

"I swear on John Flint's black heart that we have a twenty-minute truce!" He waited for the younger man to move. "Well, don't just stand out there in the rain!"

"Thank you, Captain!" Henry ran to the steps and up onto the porch where he shook like a dog and blew the weather from his nose on the white cloth. "I'm cold and I could sure use a draft of rum."

Joshua backed away to let the lad pass. "There's towels in the pantry and then meet me in my study."

"Thank you, Captain." Henry was back in a minute and spotted the stack of money on the desk. "Does that money have something to do with the governor?"

"Yes—a bribe to buy me a letter of marque." Joshua poured two glasses of rum. "Before we get to this thing you want to tell me about, tell me where you went and what you've been doing since I tried to kill you in New York."

"Here and there."

"Where is here and there?"

"Being the pickpocket that I am, I mostly stayed around rich people who owned things that needed stealing." He picked up his glass and took a large gulp. "A person does whatever he must to eat and stay warm."

"Your time is running out, Henry. I have a man to kill, so get to it!"

"Oh? And who might this walking corpse be?"

"John Paul Jones, but you wouldn't know him."

"And what did this John Paul Jones do to you that has earned him this fate?"

"Okay." Joshua gave a huff. "After I dug up John Flint's body and threw it to the crabs, we went out in *Seacrest*, looking for a prize ship for the merchants of Savannah. We came upon a merchantman named *Amazing Grace* out of Edinburgh, Scotland that was bound for Charles Town. The Brits were blockading Savannah, so we took the ship to Kings Town and traded it and *Seacrest* to Charles Noble for *Le Tiburon*."

"Then what?"

"Word got back to me the a few days later that there were a thousand carronades hid in the bilge as ballast."

"Then what?"

"Charles Noble wouldn't give them back, so I set out to take his son hostage to force his hand."

"Let me guess. David Noble was sailing to Fredericksburg with John Paul Jones, you got into a shooting battle with them near Savannah, and they got lucky and took off your rudder."

"How do you know about that?"

"After the pickpocketing, I was hired as a carpenter at the Forrestal Shipyard up in Charles Town. That's where I heard the whole story." Henry looked to the money on the desk. "By the bye, you never paid me for that trip to New York." He reached across and put his hand on the money. "This looks to be about what you owe—"

Before he could finish the words, Joshua pulled his knife and plunged it into the soft flesh between Henry's thumb and palm, pinning him to the money and the desk.

"Belay!" Henry screamed as he watched the blood begin to run from under his hand onto the money. "I need that hand for digging treasure!"

"What treasure?" Smoot gave the knife a slight twist. "Out with it!"

"That's what I'm here for, Captain!" Henry looked down at his pinioned hand. "Release my hand and I'll tell you!"

"No!" Joshua held the knife firm. "Tell me about this treasure, or I might just take your whole hand off."

"Okay, but I want five shares of whatever treasure we bring back."

"That's captain's pay!" Smoot shook his head. "I only get five shares myself!"

"That may be, Captain, but my share will be the same as yours, or I'll go my way and you can find your own treasure."

"And just so that I can speculate on the matter, how much money will these five shares bring you?"

"No!" Henry gave a pained grimace. "First, you pull your knife from my hand!"

"Hmm." Smoot was interested, and figured he could always kill Henry later when the time was right. "Tell you what, Henry." He pulled the knife free, wiped the blood on the rain-soaked towel, and set it aside. "If my crew agrees, and mind you they're not likely—"

"Don't give me that bilge water!" Henry held up his hand and let some of his blood drip onto the desk. He dipped a finger into the crimson paint and began to draw an outline. He stopped and looked up. "Your crew does exactly what you tell them!"

"If I agree—"

"It's yes or it's no—nothing in between!"

Smoot studied the unfinished outline for a moment. "That's John Silver's map—the one we took to New York! That's the island they call Dead Man's Chest."

"Aye, Captain Smoot." He gave Joshua a toothy grin. "It's a million and a half in Spanish treasure."

"So, *that's* what John Silver wanted." Joshua thought for a moment. "All right, you can have your shares but—"

"All five?"

"Yes, all five of everything we take, just like me." Smoot leaned forward and spoke slowly. "But, if we set sail and this turns out to be like New York, I'll have your heart for supper!"

"It's no lie, Captain." Henry dipped his finger in the blood again, finished the outline, and gave it a tap. "I just finished painting the names on the sterns of two identical brigs that Alex Forrestal and his group of patriots have built so they can sail to Dead Man's Chest to dig up the other two-thirds of Captain Rip Rap's treasure."

"Why identical ships?"

"One will sail to Kings Town to retrieve their cannons, and the other one will sail to Dead Man's Chest for the treasure."

"But if they already know that Charles has their cannons—"

"It's a three-way deal." Henry held up his uninjured hand. "The treasure will be paid to Charles Noble for his cannons."

"Go on."

"That's it. The two ships will meet near the Bahama Islands, the crews will switch, and each ship will go its own way." He gave a smile. "Long John Silver will finally get his treasure, and the Americans will get the cannons they were smuggling from Scotland to fight the Brits."

"You said it's a three-way deal. What's the third thing?"

"John Paul Jones—the man who took off *Le Tiburon*'s rudder—will lead the expedition to Dead Man's Chest, and when the Americans get their cannons, he will be rewarded with a naval commission."

"Show me." Smoot put the tip of his knife inside the bloody outline. "Show me where they'll be digging."

"Nobody but Robert Ormerod knows that." Henry looked at his wound. "As I understand it, Ormerod will not disclose the location until the *Silver Cloud* is safe and ready to take the treasure aboard."

"The Yorkman is sailing with them?"

"Yes, and the only reason he's doing it is for patriotism—so America can break away from England."

"Tell me more about these two ships they're building."

"They began as brigs, but when Captain Jones presented his plan, Mister Forrestal made some important changes to them."

"What changes?"

"They're calling them frigates."

"Frigates?"

"They told me the name means a full-rigged ship much like the French men-of-war."

"Tell me about these ships—their tonnage, length, number of guns—everything you can remember."

"They're 43 feet at the beam, 175 feet at the waterline, 1,400 tons displacement, and they can put up over 42,000 square feet of sails." He paused. "Oh, and they carry 36 guns that are hid behind thin sheets of wood to make them look like unarmed merchantmen."

"How soon will these two *Silver Clouds* depart from Charles Town?"

"In a fortnight."

Smoot sat back and rubbed the afternoon stubble on his chin. "Besides you and me, how many others know about this secret mission?"

"Only a guess, but there's Alexander Forrestal, Robert Ormerod, Captain Jones, David Noble, and a Dutchman named Jack Van Mourik." He paused. "And I'm sure all the men who pooled their money to pay for those cannons."

"David Noble?" Joshua sat back and closed his eyes as he remembered his battle with the *Falmouth Packet*. "And just how, pray tell, did you—a lowly carpenter—find out about this secret plan?"

"Jack Van Mourik told me." Henry smiled. "Took me a whole bottle of rum to loosen his tongue, but he told me everything." Henry leaned forward. "That's why I am here. All we have to do is get there before the *Silver Cloud* and watch when they start digging."

"And will this *Silver Cloud* be sailing alone?"

"Van Mourik told me that a privateer captain named Alan Steele will sail ahead in the fourteen-gun privateer *Eagle* to be waiting for them at Christiansted."

"And you're certain that Robert Ormerod will be aboard the *Silver Cloud*?"

"I saw Mister Ormerod at the shipyard." Henry nodded. "He's going with them." Henry waited while Joshua fell into deep contemplation. After several minutes, Henry broke the silence. "What's the matter?"

"You know, Henry…"

"What?"

"It sure would be a help if you could go back and get yourself on the crew of the treasure ship. Could you do that?"

"No. The moment Ormerod recognizes me, I'd be strung up for killing his little girl."

"Since you brought it up, Henry, how did that happen?"

"I don't know."

"But you were watching her. How could you not see the fire start, and how could you let her die?"

"I was with the girl you sent to me."

"What girl?"

"Daisy. She told me that you paid for her, for the room, and for the rum we shared."

"I didn't do that."

"Well, somebody did." Henry gave a squint. "Somebody knew what we were doing and sent that girl to distract me so he could set that fire."

"Then Ormerod had an enemy in New York—somebody who wanted revenge and wanted us to take the blame."

"Does this change things between us, Captain?"

"Yes." Joshua tapped the bloody outline. "Since you can't go back, I'll arrange for one of my best men to go up to Charles Town to get on that crew."

"But the crew was already full before I left the place."

"Then my man will have to kill one of them and get hired in his place."

ABOUT THE AUTHOR

Commander Roger L Johnson was born in Los Angeles, California on January 29, 1944. At age nineteen, he was chosen for pilot training at the prestigious Naval Air Training Command where he graduated as the top student from his 57-man class. After three cruises to Vietnam aboard the aircraft carriers Ticonderoga, Enterprise, and Midway, Roger joined the fire service while remaining in the Naval Air Reserves. In 2001, he completed a 28-year career as a Crew Captain with Cal Fire at Klamath, California. Along with his extensive writing endeavors, Roger worked as a cartoonist for three separate magazine publishers. He is now known as the "Turtleman of Gig Harbor," having made and given away nearly a thousand turtles made from stones found on the beach. He and his wife Elizabeth live in Gig Harbor, Washington where he continues to write and create.

Made in the USA
Columbia, SC
20 November 2024

46511432R00100